OyMG

Amy Fellner Dominy

Walker & Company ✹ New York

Copyright © 2011 by Amy Fellner Dominy

First published in the United States of America in May 2011
by Walker Publishing Company, Inc., a division of Bloomsbury Publishing, Inc.
www.bloomsburyteens.com

For information about permission to reproduce selections from this book, write to
Permissions, Walker BFYR, 175 Fifth Avenue, New York, New York 10010

Library of Congress Cataloging-in-Publication Data
Dominy, Amy Fellner.
OyMG / Amy Fellner Dominy.
p.   cm.
Summary: Fourteen-year-old Ellie will do almost anything to win a scholarship to the best
speech school in the country, but must decide if she is willing to hide her Jewish heritage while
at a Phoenix, Arizona, summer camp that could help her reach her goal.
ISBN 978-0-8027-2177-8
[1. Camps—Fiction.   2. Debates and debating—Fiction.   3. Public speaking—Fiction.
4. Prejudices—Fiction.   5. Jews—Arizona—Fiction.   6. Individuality—Fiction.
7. Arizona—Fiction.]   I. Title.
PZ7.D71184Oym 2011   [Fic]—dc22   2010034581

Book design by Danielle Delaney
Typeset by Westchester Book Composition
Printed in the U.S.A. by Quad/Graphics, Fairfield, Pennsylvania
2 4 6 8 10 9 7 5 3 1

For Rachel and Kyle,
and in memory of my dad, Irving W. Fellner

OyMG

CHAPTER 1

I love to argue. I'll argue about anything—school uniforms, raising the driving age, or ear hair. I can be for something or against it—doesn't matter. That's why my speech coach says I'm such a natural. Mom and Dad say I was born to argue. My first word was "no" and fourteen years later, it's still my favorite. That's how I knew something was different about Devon Yeats. I took one look at him and all I wanted to say was . . . yes.

I met Devon the first day of the Christian Society Speech and Performing Arts camp. CSSPA is one of the best summer camps for incoming freshmen who want to compete on their high school speech and debate teams. When I got my acceptance letter, I was so psyched. Zeydeh, my grandpa, said I was *meshugah ahf toit*. Roughly translated, that's Yiddish for "crazy as a loon."

"What Jewish girl goes to a Christian camp?" he ranted.

"*Speech and debate* camp," I said.

"We've been arguing with Christians for two thousand years. You have to go to camp to argue more?"

I was watching him chop onions in the kitchen. Zeydeh has his own house down the street, but most nights he cooks for us. "It has nothing to do with religion," I said. "The camp is held at Benedict's High School and it's open to anyone. The Christian Society is just the sponsor."

He waved his knife in the air. "That's what they tell you, Ellie. Next thing you know, you're genuflecting and craving little wafers."

"That's Catholic, Zeydeh."

"*Hoomf.*"

Hoomf was Zeydeh's version of a sarcastic grunt. Combined with an eye roll, it was his standard answer when he had no answer. It meant, "I'm right because I say I'm right." That's why I hated arguing with Zeydeh. It was like arguing with a crazy person.

Correction. It *was* arguing with a crazy person.

"It's an honor even to get in," I told him. "I had to write an essay and get a letter of recommendation just to apply. Besides," I added, "it's the only way I can get into Benedict's."

His fingers were stiff and bent with arthritis, but he still worked the knife like an expert. "And Benedict's is such a good school?"

"The best," I said. "Their speech team travels all over the country. This past year, they went to tourneys in Dallas and Chicago and at Harvard. They sweep State every year, and last year, they qualified sixteen students to Nationals. Sixteen!"

I squished a piece of onion between my fingers. "That's huge, Zeydeh. Once you make Nationals, you're like a rock star for life."

I wasn't sure yet what I wanted to be—famous litigator, feared lobbyist, president of the world—but I was going to be *something*. And it all started with Benedict's.

Officially, it was called Benedict's Conservatory of Arts and Academics. Just the name gave me goose bumps. I'd tried applying, but Benedict's was a private school and impossible to get into unless you were rich or connected. Which I wasn't. I'd registered to start my freshman year at Canyon View High in August, but I was praying I could still get into Benedict's. Camp was my one shot. Every year, one or two of the top finishers at CSSPA were offered a private scholarship. If I could kick butt at camp, I'd bypass the Benedict's waiting list and get full tuition.

"Even Mom and Dad think the camp is a great idea," I said.

"*Hoomf*," he grunted again. "Your parents think Cheez Whiz is a great idea—what do they know?"

"They know everything is not about religion." If they thought like Zeydeh, my parents wouldn't even have gotten married, since Mom is Jewish and Dad is Christian. "Forget it," I said. "I'm not arguing with you."

"Who's arguing?"

"Then wish me luck."

"Don't I always?" His eyes flashed at me beneath his curly gray eyebrows. He had the same curly gray hair on his head—and poking out from inside his ears.

"This camp will help you reach your dreams?" he asked, his expression suddenly serious.

"If I do well, yeah."

"Then you should go." He set down the knife and wiped his hands. "Always you should follow your dreams."

And Benedict's was my dream. Canyon View would be okay. But at Benedict's, I'd be with the best of the best. I'd *be* one of the best.

Zeydeh rubbed the back of one hand over my cheek. His skin was soft and papery. As familiar as my own. "Always remember, my Eleanor Jane. You can do anything. Be anything."

I wrapped my arms around his waist until I felt the bony knobs of his spine and smelled the starch of his shirt and the vanilla scent that is Zeydeh. I squeezed him and pressed closer until there was no room for anything between us. "I love you, Zeydeh."

"I love you, too," he said. "But if men wearing purple robes try to sprinkle water on your forehead, run!"

◇

Even as a kid, I knew Zeydeh was different. For one thing, we didn't call him Grandpa like a normal grandfather—we called him Zeydeh, the Yiddish word for grandfather. And he didn't act normal. Grandma and Grandpa Taylor, my dad's parents, took me and my brother, Benny, for pizza, read us stories about bunnies, and when I asked why the neighbor's dog had two tails, they told me to hush.

Zeydeh taught us to cuss in Yiddish, he baked cookies for breakfast, and when I asked about the dog, he demanded to see it. Then, he explained the dog had one tail and one penis. You're not supposed to say "penis" to kids, but Zeydeh didn't care. He'll say anything to anyone. He still talks to Bubbe, my grandma, even though she's been dead for eight years. According to him, why should death get in the way of a good conversation?

Zeydeh loves a good conversation. And I inherited his gift of gab. Jews have always been great orators, he says—Maimonides, Einstein, Jerry Seinfeld. I'm following in their footsteps—another Jew to carry on the tradition.

For Zeydeh, being Jewish isn't just a religion. It's life and death. Bubbe lost an uncle, an aunt, and three cousins in the Holocaust. So that's big. It haunts Zeydeh. And I get it, I really do. But sometimes he forgets: This isn't Nazi Germany. This isn't the 1940s. This is boring, hotter-than-jalapeños Phoenix, Arizona. It's the twenty-first century. It's a four-week, six-hours-a-day speech and performing arts summer camp.

And Zeydeh was worried for nothing.

CHAPTER 2

The morning that camp began, I woke with my fingers clenched around my sheets. My mind was still fuzzy from a too-real dream. Me on stage at a speech tourney. I wore a blue suit with shiny red boots. Sitting across from me was Jesus. He had a crown of thorns on his head and when he crossed his legs, his white robes rode up his calves. He wore Nike high-tops with rainbow laces. Then he opened his mouth to talk, but Zeydeh's New-York-Jew accent came out. "So, you want to argue?"

I shuddered and sat up in bed.

"You okay?"

I screeched, then realized it wasn't Jesus standing at my bedroom door with a cup of coffee. It was my mom in a long white bathrobe. "How long have you been there?" I asked.

"Only a minute," she said in her scratchy morning voice. "I was going to wake you, but you had such a strange look on your face."

"A dream," I muttered. I ran a hand through my hair, which wasn't easy with all the knots. It made me crazy. During the day, my hair was completely straight—it hung halfway down my neck and refused to hold a curl. But at night, it tangled into knots only half a bottle of conditioner would unravel.

"Want to tell me?" my mom coaxed.

"It was a speech tournament and I was competing against Jesus."

The corners of her mouth twitched up as she sat down beside me. "Was he any good?"

"He had hairy legs and he sounded like Zeydeh."

"Really?" She sipped her coffee. "You should tell Zeydeh you're dreaming about Jesus."

"You want to kill him?" I laughed at the look on her face. "Don't answer that."

Mom likes to say Zeydeh is her cross to bear. She says it even though she's Jewish, even though crosses are a Christian thing. She's just trying to make Zeydeh mad. He thinks our home should be more Jewish, even though the only thing Christian in it is Dad. Zeydeh raised Mom as a heavy-duty Jew, but Mom rebelled, and then she fell in love with Dad. A Christian. Or, as Zeydeh says, a goy—a non-Jew. As in, "Oy, she married a goy."

"Be nice to him today," I said. "He's been looking kind of pale."

"Is he drinking his juice every morning?"

"He says he is."

She sighed. "As if we can trust him. When your brother wakes up, I'll send him down to check on Zeydeh. Maybe I'll make an appointment with the doctor."

"Don't tell him I said anything."

She smiled and rubbed my arm. "Don't worry. He'll be fine."

I glanced over at a gray velvet jewelry box on my bedside table. "He gave me Bubbe's necklace to wear to camp."

"Her Jewish star?" Mom's eyebrows lifted. "Wow. Be careful with that. He rarely parts with it."

"Probably thinks it'll ward off evil."

We both grinned.

"I'm so excited for you, Ellie," she said, her eyes shining. Mom has great eyes—honey brown, thick lashes, and a beautiful oval shape. I got the honey brown color and thick lashes, but instead of oval, mine are round. I always look surprised.

"You're going to have an amazing experience," she said. "You'll meet kids from all over the state."

"The best of the best." I sat up, the mattress squeaking under my hands.

"And you'll make lifelong friends," she added. "I met Sally Harris at a camp when I was your age."

"I'm not there to make friends, Mom." I rolled my eyes. "I'm there to demolish the competition and win a scholarship."

"Isn't that friendly." She made a face and swatted my hip. "You'd better get ready. The Swans will be here soon to pick you up."

◇

Megan Swan is my best friend. I met her in first grade—the alphabet brought us together. Swan followed by Taylor. If Mom had married someone named Applegate, I would have stood next to Hannah Arlen, who got expelled in third grade for setting a fire in the teachers' lounge. Instead, I lined up that first day and Megan lined up in front of me.

I call it The Year of No Hair. I had fallen asleep chewing a wad of gum and woken up wearing it on my head like a sticky pink helmet. Mom had to shave my head. She bought me a blond wig with curls that never moved. Not even when I stood under a ceiling fan on full blast. I wore my wig that first day and pretended I looked like a movie star, not an alien.

Then the girl ahead of me sucked in a breath through crooked teeth and asked, "Is your hair fake?"

I balled up my hands and glared at her the way Zeydeh had showed me, with squinty eyes and thin lips. But she didn't look like a bully. She had thick glasses, a pointy chin, and frizzy hair the color of dirt that seemed to grow out, not down.

"It's Twinkie yellow," she said, looking enviously at my wig. "I love Twinkies. Do you think I could get one with braids?"

I like to say I recognized a kindred spirit. Mostly, I recognized someone with hair problems nearly as bad as mine. From that day on, we were best friends.

Megan loves theater the way I love speech. She's good, too; she has a way of disappearing into her characters so you forget it's even her. She registered for Benedict's but she says she'll go wherever I go. Megan doesn't have to worry about a scholarship or getting accepted. Her parents already got her in the old-fashioned way: with tons of cash.

I was waiting outside when Mr. Swan pulled into our driveway. I climbed into his car with a little sigh of happiness. Megan's dad drove a gold Lexus with leather seats, tinted windows, and surround-sound speakers. Plus, he traded in his cars every nine months, so the leather always had that new-car smell.

We'd go home at the end of the day Taylor-style—stuffed in the backseat of my dad's pickup truck. Dad owns a landscaping business, which usually means bags of potting soil around our feet and nose plugs in September when he stocks up on fertilizer for the winter grass. Mom drives a VW wagon. It loses points for style, but at least it's comfortable. Unfortunately, she teaches summer school to fifth graders, so Dad has pick-up duty in the pickup.

"Nice," Megan said, looking me over. "Professional with a dash of sexy."

I'd worn a blue tank that met the three-finger rule (tank-top straps must be wider than three fingers), with white crop pants and sandals that showed off my pink toenails. Megan, on the other hand, was obviously going for something different.

"What do you call your look?" I asked. "Homeless Chic?"

I shielded my eyes from her shirt and she laughed. It was neon yellow, three sizes too big, and hung over hideous green doctor pants. She wore gray Converse sneakers with yellow laces. Her hair, which turned into a cloud of frizz if it grew past her ears, was too short to put up. But she'd stuck three yellow clips through her bangs. Megan didn't have great beauty, but she did have great style. You just never knew which style it would be.

Sunlight caught the wires of her braces and the orange rubber bands glowed like a jack-o'-lantern. I'd finished with braces more than a year ago, but Megan had to wait for jaw realignment. She actually liked the braces—said they added to her "persona." Megan was all about persona—she was constantly recreating herself, just like a character from a play.

"I think you misunderstood when Coach said you should get into character," I told her. "He didn't mean permanently."

She ignored me, adjusting two bracelets of yellow beads. "Speaking of Coach, you remember what he said?"

Coach was Mr. Joyce—the speech-team adviser and drama teacher at our middle school. He'd written the letters of recommendation for us to get into camp. We hadn't asked for his "keys to success" but Coach couldn't resist.

"What are you going to do, girls?" I barked in my best gravelly Coach voice.

"Stand up! Stand out! Stand firm!" Megan barked back.

We laughed and slapped a high five. I settled back in my cushy seat. As Coach liked to say, nothing stood in our way but ourselves.

But Coach had never met Devon Yeats.

CHAPTER 3

I noticed him during orientation. Or, actually, Megan did.

We'd signed in at the front lobby and been given "Christian Society—Faith in the World" name tags to smack on our shirts. Then we were directed to the auditorium for an assembly. I couldn't stop looking around. Benedict's was the nicest school I'd ever seen. The floors were tiled in different shades of tan and brown, and the walls were cream with dark wood molding along the ceiling. It smelled like wood polish and everything gleamed—even the classroom doors.

The school had been here for sixty years, but it didn't feel old in a run-down way. It felt old in a rich way. The campus itself was off a main street in the downtown area, but it was tucked back behind a screen of old trees. The front courtyard had a fountain, ceramic statues on pedestals, and cobblestone walkways leading to the main doors. I actually wiped my sandals on the mat before I walked in. It just felt *different*.

Like everything else at Benedict's, the auditorium was amazing. There were movie theater chairs with blue seat cushions, a stage with full-length curtains, and hanging lights. At Canyon View, the cafeteria doubled as a stage, and you got metal folding chairs to sit on. Even the air at Benedict's smelled better. I could get used to this.

A woman stood behind a podium on the stage, but we ignored her and checked out the other campers. Most of the kids were dressed like me, only with better logos over their chests and their butts. I saw one girl toss down a blinged-out backpack that must have cost more than my clothing allowance for the year. Someday, I'd have enough money to trash nice things, too.

Megan rolled up her sleeves as she looked around. "Not bad," she whispered. "Definite potential."

There were about eighty kids, I guessed, more girls than guys. Not that Megan was wasting time on the girls. She had an internal radar system for a certain type of guy. Unfortunately, not the tall, dark, handsome type that might have come in handy. She went for the intense, brooding, angry guy who wore black everything, snapped rubber bands against his wrist, and looked slightly twisted. If he had a book of poetry or something depressing from the AP list— even better.

"Check him," Megan breathed, nudging my shoulder. "Two rows up, far right."

I looked. Then looked again. *Holy crap.* The guy was definitely intense, as in *intensely hot.* He was sitting at an angle, talking to the guy next to him. He had short, black hair with that perfectly messy look. Squarish face, tanned skin, nice lips, and the arm that hung over the back of his seat had actual muscle attached. If he had nice teeth, he'd be a perfect ten.

Megan leaned closer. "Isn't he—"

"Hot!"

Megan's surprised eyes shifted to my face. "Please! He's probably as fake as my mom's boobs."

"Then why are you scoping him out?"

"Because that's Devon Yeats."

I sucked in a breath. "You mean—"

"Doris Yeats is his grandmother."

I leaned forward, my heart quickening. Doris Yeats was the private donor who funded the Benedict's Scholarship. There would be a panel of judges to determine who won my oratory event, but Mrs. Yeats would determine who won an all-expenses-paid trip to Benedict's in the fall. "How do you know that's Devon?" I asked.

"I met him at a charity event last Christmas."

Megan's mom was the queen of charity events. Not because she liked helping people, according to Megan, but because she loved to dress up and schmooze.

"You didn't tell me that!"

"It was for all of two seconds. My mom insisted." Megan rolled her eyes. "I didn't pay much attention. He lives with his mom in Chicago or somewhere. He was just visiting for winter break."

"So what's he doing here now?"

"I don't know. My mom said something about Devon's dad dying a few years back and how Mrs. Yeats wanted Devon and his mom to move to Phoenix. Maybe she talked them into it. Or maybe he's just here for summer camp. Supposedly, he's big into speech team. He's in oratory, by the way."

"My event? Is he any good?" I slanted another look at him. He was too pretty to be smart.

"According to Granny Yeats, who bragged about him the entire time, he was practically unbeatable. Junior high stud. Four first-place finishes, blah, blah, blah . . ."

"Blah, blah, blah?" I repeated. "This is my competition and that's all you can remember?"

"I didn't know he'd show up here."

I lifted the hair off my neck and fanned cool air against my skin for a second. "What about Doris Yeats? Is she here?" I'd Googled as much info about her as I could. She had bazillions from a business her husband had sold before he died. As far as I could tell, her official job now was Charity Do-Gooder—and her favorite cause was Benedict's. She was on the school board, plus benefactor of the speech program. Google had turned up a picture of her at some charity dinner, but I wasn't sure I'd recognize her in person.

I waited while Megan looked around. "I don't see her. She's got silver hair and walks like there's a stick up her butt."

I glanced around the edge of the auditorium where the adults had gathered. "I want to introduce myself as soon as I can."

"First impressions," Megan muttered.

"Exactly." Doris Yeats had a rep for being tough. Supposedly, she spared everyone five minutes of her time, and then made up her mind. Your first impression could be your last.

"So what did you think of Devon?" I asked.

Megan looked in his direction again. "He seemed nice enough for a guy born with a perfect face. Wait until you see his eyes. They're amazing."

I shrugged, unconvinced. The last time Megan said that, the guy in question turned out to have a lazy eye. She dated him for two months. Devon could have *three* eyes and Megan would call that amazing, too.

"Welcome to CSSPA." The pinched voice flooded the auditorium. Megan and I turned to the stage. The lady paused until everyone quieted down. "I am Mrs. Clancy, camp director." Mrs. Clancy looked like she'd gotten up on the wrong side of the bed and fallen into a vat of lemons. Her mouth puckered into a circle of wrinkles as she talked.

"You should all have your schedules with group and room assignments. Other than assembly each morning, where we'll share announcements and prayer, you will be spending your days with your group. Lunch will be held in the cafeteria from 12:00 to 12:45."

I glanced at Megan, my mouth puckered into a tiny *o*, but she'd puckered, too. We both sputtered a little, trying not to laugh.

"When we break," Mrs. Clancy continued, "you'll please move quickly to your rooms. Your instructors are anxious to begin. Now, if you'll bow your heads, in Jesus's name we pray."

Here it was, as advertised—daily prayer. It was actually part of the syllabus. Zeydeh had loved that. But I also showed him the place on the website that said applicants of all religions were welcome. And no one said I had to pray.

I kept my head up and looked around. Mrs. Clancy started saying something Jesus-y. I figured there would be other kids looking around, but all I saw were necks . . . lots of bent necks. I shifted in my seat, wishing she'd finish already. It felt weird. Christians thought Jesus was the son of God, but Jews thought he was a man. So listening to prayers in the name of Jesus made me feel traitorous to God.

And Zeydeh. I sighed. If he could see me now, it would kill him.

Again.

◇

The first time Zeydeh died, I was five years old.

Zeydeh didn't actually die in Aisle 12 of Fry's grocery store—but Mom thought he had. It was the summer before I started kindergarten. Bubbe had died a few months before, and Zeydeh had gone into a depression. He'd always loved to cook, but now he wouldn't even eat. Mom would take him with us to the grocery store, thinking he'd get interested in food again.

That day, Benny and I were with Mom in the frozen foods aisle. Benny was strapped in Mom's cart, and I was wheeling my toy cart around her legs. Zeydeh had gone to look at the pasta. Next thing we knew, a woman started to shriek from across the store. I'm not even sure how Mom knew. But she did.

When we careened around the corner of Aisle 12, there he was. Sprawled flat on the linoleum, a trail of red bleeding from his forehead to the floor. I remember thinking that only Zeydeh would die in a grocery store. He wouldn't even die like a regular grandpa.

Then the screaming started.

It took me a minute to realize it was coming from my own mother. I'd only ever seen her fight with Zeydeh, but now she dropped to her knees beside me. Her whole face sort of caved in on itself. She screamed and sobbed as if she could raise the dead. And she did.

Because suddenly Zeydeh woke up. Turned out the "pool of blood" was Prego marinara. He'd fainted with a jar of spaghetti sauce in his hand, and it had splattered everywhere. He had a gash on one arm from the broken glass, but other than that, the paramedic said he was fine.

Mom said otherwise. She took Zeydeh to the doctor and found out he had hypotension, which means low blood pressure. He had to take better care of himself and drink plenty of liquids, or he'd be susceptible to dizziness and could end up fainting again. The doctor said mornings were especially dangerous because blood pressure could decrease overnight. So Mom said Zeydeh couldn't be alone so much. She said every morning one of us would go to his house and make sure he drank a big glass of juice. Usually, that someone was me.

Nine years later, I could still picture him dead on the floor

18

◇◇◇◇◇

of Fry's. It made me feel sick. Sitting in the Benedict's auditorium, I squeezed my eyes shut, and sent up my own prayer. *Dear God, please watch out for Zeydeh. And could you help me make a good first impression on Mrs. Yeats?* I paused. *And, uh, Jesus, if you're up there—nothing personal or anything.*

CHAPTER 4

When I pushed open the door to 6C, everyone stood in the back of the room and a lady was gesturing for them to make a circle. I'd hung around the auditorium as long as I could, hoping to spot Mrs. Yeats and introduce myself, but no luck. Maybe I'd see her at lunch.

I dropped my pack by a front-row desk that looked empty and took a quick glance around as I joined the circle. It was the nicest classroom I'd ever been in. The desks were a dark, polished wood with matching chairs. There was a bank of windows along the back with black and gold blinds, and walls painted to look like gold speckles. Another door in the far corner of the room was framed by posters of old presidents. A huge whiteboard covered the front wall. Written in green marker were the words "Mrs. Becca Lee, Original Oratory."

I slipped in between two girls and checked out Mrs. Lee. She looked thirty-something, with short brown hair that just cleared her ears, straight eyebrows, and intense green eyes.

"I'm Mrs. Lee, your team leader," she said in a deep, throaty voice. "I competed in speech tournaments for many years and now teach at Benedict's. According to the NFL, the National Forensic League, an original oratory is an original speech—no longer than ten minutes—about any topic you choose. The speech must be presented from memory without the use of notes or a script. Simple, right?" She raised her eyebrows, as if challenging us. "In fact, it's not simple at all."

I took a deep breath. Someone near me was sucking an orange Tic Tac—I could smell it.

"Why do some oratories break through the competition when other oratories don't?" Mrs. Lee asked. "And most importantly, how do you create the kind that will break through?" She turned slowly, her gaze locking with mine for a second before moving on. "That's what you're about to find out. By the end of this camp, you will have researched and written an original oratory. You will present your oratory on stage at our mock tournament in front of a panel of judges and compete against your peers for the privilege of calling yourself the best of CSSPA."

A current of electricity seemed to crackle around the room. Goose bumps prickled on my arms. *The best of CSSPA.* That was going to be me.

"I happen to believe in the value of performance—the

more you do, the less nervous you'll be," Mrs. Lee explained. "So, expect many opportunities to perform. In fact, let's start now with a little icebreaker."

I exchanged glances with the girl on my right. Her eyes looked huge. She twirled a piece of hair around shaky fingers.

"There are ten of you in this class," Mrs. Lee said. "You'll be working closely together as teammates as well as competitors. This exercise will give you an opportunity to get familiar with one another."

The room got so quiet I wondered if everyone was holding their breath. Even the air conditioner had kicked off into silence.

"Here's how it works," she explained. "You'll turn to the person next to you and I'll call out a topic. The person on the right can argue any position on that topic for one minute. I'll call time, and the other person will rebut the argument. After that, you'll introduce yourselves and say where you attend school. Then, I'll call time. You'll switch partners and we'll start again with a new topic. Any questions?"

I tried to hide my grin. This would be a piece of cake. I could talk for *ten* minutes and say nothing. I could do one minute in my sleep.

I turned back to the hair twirler. Her name tag read "Sarah." She was taller than me, with dirty blond hair and a nervous smile.

"The covers of glamour magazines are pornography," Mrs. Lee called out. "Go."

Sarah began with an argument about women being

turned into objects. I listened with half of my brain and plotted with the other. When it was my turn, I rebutted with freedom of speech. I was working my way into the body as art when Mrs. Lee called, "Time. Introduce yourselves, then switch."

I ruled on standardized tests with a red-headed guy named Ethan wearing a retainer that clacked when he talked. I gave an inspired rant on mandatory college against Nancy, who wore Virgin Mary earrings. When Mrs. Lee called switch for the fourth time, I turned, and there was Devon.

My heart froze, midbeat. *Holy crap.* His eyes were . . . startling.

Vaguely, I heard Mrs. Lee call out something.

His irises were the clearest, lightest blue I'd ever seen, but rimmed in a deeper blue. They looked like pools without a bottom. For once in her life, Megan had understated something.

Then Devon started talking and my brain refocused. *Uh-oh!* What was the topic?

"It can create huge limitations," Devon said. "What about work? After-school activities? If the law were changed, how many lives would be affected?"

What law? Come on, come on . . . restate the topic . . .

"Time!" Mrs. Lee called.

Crap! A blur of voices filled the room as everyone rebutted the arguments. Except me.

Devon's dark brows slanted down.

I licked my lips. I was going to have to wing this. I lifted my shoulders and tried to look taller than five feet three. Half of winning was looking like a winner.

"If I appear to be speechless," I began, in an airy voice, "it's because I am. Your argument defies logic." I planted my hands on my hips. "In fact, your argument lacks the subtle truth that I think we need to consider when we look at this, uh, issue. Because . . . this issue . . . however you might disagree, requires a thorough and complete understanding of the other issues that impact it. For instance—"

"Time!" Mrs. Lee called.

Yes! I let out a silent breath and smiled. *There. Not too bad.*

Except Devon had a funny look in his bottomless eyes, and his brows had dipped down again. "You don't know what the topic is, do you?"

My smile faded. "Of course I do." Before he could say anything else, I added, "I'm Ellie Taylor. Canyon View High School."

"Devon Yeats. Benedict's."

Benedict's? Did that mean he'd moved here for good?

Then he added, "Driving age."

I shifted on my feet. "What?"

"That was our topic. Raising the driving age to eighteen."

Heat shot through my cheeks. "I knew that."

I met his eyes, ready to stare him down. Only, he stared back. Our eyes held, and a strange shiver raced to the pit of my stomach.

"Switch," Mrs. Lee called.

I swallowed. Hard. Without looking at him again, I stepped

around Devon so fast, my shoulder brushed his. I kept my eyes forward, shook back my hair, and willed my heart to calm down. I just wasn't used to being challenged like that. I pasted on a smile for the tall, blond-haired guy who was next. "Peter," his tag read. His eyes were hazel.

But all I could see in my head were a pair of blue, blue eyes. What was my problem? I never got distracted by a pair of eyes—I didn't care how gorgeous they were. I shivered again, but this time with disgust.

While I was losing myself in Devon's eyes, I had the feeling he'd been looking right through me.

◇

I have a long and pathetic history with romance. It's not my fault. If romance worked logically, it would be a different story. But you can't argue your way into someone's heart. I know.

I've tried.

In third grade, I told Gabriel Garcia all the reasons he should like me: My hair was brown like his. I was better than him in math. No one else liked him.

He backed away like ants were crawling out my eyes.

In sixth grade, I grew wiser. I fell for Brad Willets—football hero. I went to a district board meeting and argued the school fields shouldn't be locked on weekends since taxpayers funded them. I got more playing time for Brad Willets's football team. Brad was thrilled. But Brad did not dump his girlfriend, Ashley, to invite me to the sixth-grade dance.

Megan said I couldn't force romance. It had to happen

naturally. So, when Kyle Walters, science wiz and overall nice guy, asked me if I wanted to hang out this past March, I said yes. I liked Kyle. Kyle liked me. Logically, it should have worked. But after two weeks, it fizzled out. According to Megan, that was the problem. Too much fizzle.

Or, to be exact, not enough sizzle.

For Megan, sizzle was the magic something that meant true love. You couldn't organize, plan, research, or convince someone you had sizzle. Either you had it, or you didn't. "Respect the Sizzle," Megan liked to say.

Only I wasn't the sizzle kind. So maybe I'd felt a shiver when I met Devon's eyes—but that didn't mean anything. I wasn't the weak-kneed romantic type who melted into a brainless mess just because some guy was cute. Not even if the guy was Devon Yeats and cute enough to be on a magazine cover.

That shiver meant nothing.

A shiver, I reminded myself, was the opposite of a sizzle.

CHAPTER 5

About the only thing Mom and Zeydeh agree on is the importance of family dinners. And—that Zeydeh should cook. Zeydeh is a gourmet, while Mom is still trying to perfect microwave popcorn. But tonight, she'd insisted on cooking dinner in honor of my first day of camp. Zeydeh said at least he would make a pot of matzo ball soup—homemade chicken broth with fluffy dumplings.

So the chicken breasts would be dry, the green beans would be mushy, the red potatoes would be half cooked, and the rolls would be burned on the bottom. But the soup would be great. The rich scent of carrots and chicken had spread through the house, and ever since I'd gotten home from camp, I'd been walking around sniffing and listening to my stomach growl.

Finally, Mom called us down, her face flushed from the oven with her hair pointing in six directions. She wore her hair in a bun almost every day. She said it was easier that way, but her hair was even straighter than mine. Strands kept popping loose and she was forever stuffing them back in the bun or behind her ears. Mom had natural beauty—which was lucky, because she rarely bothered to fix herself up.

Mom sat at one end of the oval table and Dad sat at the other. Dad is six feet, and the only one in our family with sandy-colored hair and blue eyes. In summer, he works outside so many hours, he gets weird tan lines from his sunglasses that make him look like a raccoon. Benny and I call him Skippy Raccoon. That's actually his name—Skip.

He loves designing yards and picking out the right mix of trees, bushes, and flowers. He has a crew who can do the planting and maintenance, but he says he likes getting his hands dirty. Which they usually are.

Benny sits next to me. He's going into seventh grade but still acts like a kindergartner. He has the curliest hair of all of us, and he slicks it back with this goop that smells like gym shorts after a week in a locker. You can always smell Benny coming.

Zeydeh sits across from Benny and me. Usually, he asks us both lots of questions about whatever, but not tonight. Tonight, he kept sipping the soup and then shaking his head. It had to be the contest. For five years, Zeydeh had been trying to win the Har Zion Cooking Contest. Har Zion is his synagogue, and he'd never finished better than second. This year, he was thinking about entering his matzo ball soup.

Mom passed me the potatoes. "So tell us—what do you think?"

"The soup is too salty," Zeydeh said.

She shot him a look. "I was asking Ellie about camp."

He shrugged. "Am I stopping you?"

She rolled her eyes and looked back at me. "So?"

"So, it was good."

"That's it? Just good?"

"Did they do the secret Christian handshake?" Zeydeh asked.

"I didn't see any handshakes."

"Exactly," he said, pointing at me with his soup spoon. "That's because it's secret."

I laughed and reached for a roll.

"Did you get recess?" Benny asked.

"Recess?" I peeled off the burned bottom. "We get forty-five minutes to eat and a ten-minute bathroom break in the afternoon."

"You're kidding," he said. "What if you've got to pee?"

"You have to sign a waiver before camp relinquishing all rights to pee."

His eyes widened a second, then narrowed. "Ha. Ha." He stabbed a piece of chicken with his fork. "Sounds lame to me."

"Anyone you recognize from speech tournaments last year?" Dad asked.

I nodded. "Yeah, a couple. You know how tournaments are. There are so many kids from different schools. Even if you break through to the later rounds, you never see everyone."

"Maybe it's the parsley," Zeydeh said, smacking his lips together. "You think it's the parsley?"

29
◇◇◇◇◇

"The soup is wonderful," Dad said.

"The parsley is perfect," I added. I slurped up another spoonful.

Zeydeh shrugged off our compliments. I'd never seen him so tense.

"So what else about the camp?" Dad asked.

Mom shoved Benny's napkin onto his lap. "Who's going to be the toughest competition?"

I took another swallow of soup and set down my spoon. "There's this guy named Devon Yeats."

Mom's eyebrows lifted. "Any relation to Doris Yeats? The one who offers the scholarship?"

I nodded. "Devon is her grandson. Apparently, he's just moved here and he's going to Benedict's next year." Megan had gotten the whole scoop from a girl in her class.

"And he's good?" Dad asked.

"That's the rumor, but it's too early to tell. He's smooth, though, I'll give him that."

"Does anyone else taste the salt, or is it only me?" Zeydeh asked.

"Would you stop already with the salt?" Mom snapped.

"Of course," Zeydeh snapped back. "Don't worry, my soup is a disaster. So what if I should lose the contest again and my name is not etched onto a plaque. Who needs immortality?"

"Zeydeh, the soup is great," I said. I showed him my empty bowl to prove it.

He shrugged halfheartedly.

Mom's bangs ruffled in the hot air she blew out. "For heaven's sake," she muttered.

"If you want, you can come and watch me perform during lunch this Friday," I offered. "We're doing a mini–mock tournament. I'm not sure what it's about, but parents are welcome."

"I wish I could," Mom said. "I'll be teaching summer school."

Dad smiled at me. "The rest of us will be there. Right, Benny?"

"What?" Benny mumbled around a mouthful of food. "Who said I was coming?"

"Of course you're coming," Zeydeh said. "We'll all go."

Benny groaned and slouched in his chair.

"It'll be fun," Dad said. "We can see this Devon Yeats in action."

Against my will, Devon's eyes flashed in my mind . . . that moment when we'd locked eyes.

Mom suddenly leaned toward me. "Are you cold?"

"What?" I blinked. "No. Why?"

She rubbed my shoulder. "I could've sworn you just shivered."

"Salt," Zeydeh muttered. "It must be the salt."

CHAPTER 6

"Not again," Sarah muttered from the corner of her mouth. One finger had already snaked around a chunk of hair and was twisting nervously.

I'd taken my same front-row seat this morning, and ended up next to Sarah. She'd seemed fine until Mrs. Lee announced an impromptu speech. Now, she was the color of the whiteboard.

"You okay?" I whispered while Mrs. Lee pulled stuff out of her briefcase.

"I hate impromptu. We'll have to give a speech with hardly any time to think. That's why I'm in oratory. So I can *prepare*."

After we'd taken notes for almost two hours, a chance to give a speech sounded like fun to me. But I felt bad for Sarah, even if she was a competitor.

Mrs. Lee faced us again, only now she held a letter-sized envelope. "One of the things we discussed this morning was how every oratory should have a purpose. Are you trying to inform, to persuade, or to entertain?" She wiggled the envelope. "In here, I've got index cards with impromptu topics written on them. These topics, by the way, were all used at speech tournaments last year. You'll pick a card, and I'll tell you your goal. Then, you'll have three minutes to prepare a two-minute speech on your subject." She paused. "We'll start with Sarah, then go around the room and finish with Ellie."

Sarah flashed me a panicked look.

"You'll be great," I mouthed, wondering how white she could get before passing out.

"Even though this is an impromptu speech," Mrs. Lee added, "it still requires the same elements as an oratory: a strong opening, supporting arguments, and a summation." She held out the envelope to Sarah.

With one hand, Sarah twirled a piece of hair; with the other, she picked a card. I got a quick look at it; the words were written in big block letters: ICE CREAM.

"Your goal," Mrs. Lee said, "is to persuade us you need more of it."

Cool topic, if you asked me—but Sarah still looked freaked. Her panicked gaze darted back to me again. She'd also applied for the Benedict's Scholarship, which meant hers was one of the butts I was planning to kick. But . . . oh, what the heck. Before she looked away, I leaned forward and mouthed "calcium."

Then she moved to the center of the room, turned her back to us, and curled in her shoulders like a snail. Three minutes later, she launched into how teens weren't getting enough calcium. The solution—more ice cream. She was good, too. Smart. Organized. Hid her nerves well. I wondered if I shouldn't have helped her. But when she sat down and shot me a smile, I shot her one back. I'd still kick her butt when it mattered.

Next was Peter Burrows: Blond hair, hazel eyes—followed by the smell of oranges. Tic Tac guy, I guessed. He was a Benedict's kid, I remembered. Dressed like it, too—polo shirt tucked into khaki shorts with a belt. Peter had to entertain us about movies. He did a thing about sticky floors. Very funny, but a little hard to understand. He talked fast and swallowed the last consonant of most words. Either that, or he still had a Tic Tac in his mouth.

Then Tim Fielding: Buzz cut, glasses, red canvas sneakers. Funny, but no organization. His topic was TV, and he jumped from reality shows to 3-D technology.

Tammy Fong went next: Black hair in a pony, Q-tip skinny, very sharp, but a weak voice.

Nancy Moreno: Curly brown hair, short. Silver cross earrings today. So much energy you'd swear she just drank a Red Bull. She rushed through an informative speech on summer camps.

Kim Perry: Huge brown eyes like a puppy, white cardigan over a green dress. Soft voice but very e-mo-tion-al. Probably wrote tearjerker oratories.

Ethan Reynolds: Red-haired retainer-clacker, but did a good job on why speech team should be mandatory in high school.

Andrew Sawyer: Buttoned-up brown shirt over brown

shorts, serious expression, nervous delivery—but he might be better with a prepared speech.

Next up, Devon Yeats. I straightened in my chair as he strode up to the front and picked an index card. He had the same Benedict's look as Peter, only his polo was hanging loose over navy cargo shorts. "Toothpaste," he said, announcing his topic.

"Entertain," Mrs. Lee said.

He didn't curl up like Sarah. He didn't pace like Tim or Nancy. He didn't chew his lip like Andrew. He slid his hands into his pockets and sat on the edge of the table. I was torn between admiring him and wanting him to screw up. Then he stood and began.

"When I was five years old, I fell in love with paste. I didn't know there was a special type for teeth. I liked to eat all kinds."

Crap. He had charm, too. Before I could help it, he'd sucked me into his speech, into his humor—into him.

And those eyes. Those stupid blue eyes made you want to believe him. He rolled to a close and it was obvious to me and everyone else in the class: Devon was the guy to beat.

As he walked back to his seat, he flashed me a look. Like a smirk, only with his eyes. I turned my head away but couldn't keep my jaw from clenching. I'd stood by him this morning while Mrs. Lee opened the classroom door. I'd even looked him in the eye to prove I could without having a brain fade. He'd been talking to Peter, but when he walked by me, he whispered something in my ear. It took me a minute to realize what he'd said: "Driving age."

◇◇◇◇◇

I'd rolled my eyes at his perfect back. Let him enjoy it while he could. I'd show him.

And this was my chance.

I walked to the front table, smoothing my cranberry tank over the top of my denim skirt. Mrs. Lee smiled and held out the envelope. "Your goal will be to persuade."

I shook back my bangs and pulled a card from the envelope. The words stared up at me like a joke. A really bad joke.

"Your topic, Ellie?" Mrs. Lee asked.

My fingers curled around the card, crunching it in a fist I couldn't control. "Christmas trees: real versus fake."

◇

It's not like I've never seen a Christmas tree. You'd have to go blind from October to January to miss them. Megan alone had three Christmas trees every year—her mom paid someone to decorate them. But we never had one in our house. Dad might have been born and raised Lutheran, but he'd agreed to raise Benny and me Jewish. So we had Hanukkah—menorahs and dreidels and latkes to eat.

Once I asked Dad if he minded giving up Christmas. But he said Christmas was really about family, and helping others, and you could do that no matter what holiday you observed. Grandma Taylor heard that, and she said Christmas was really about the birth of Jesus. Then Dad said many scholars believe Jesus was most likely born in the fall, so what's the point of celebrating his birthday in December? That made Grandma Taylor mad.

As much as Zeydeh wants us to be Jewish, Grandma Taylor wants us to be Christian. It might have been a problem for us, but they live in Virginia and only visit once a year—at Easter. Still, Grandma Taylor used to read us books about Jesus and tell us about heaven for kids who believed in him. She still has us paint eggs every Easter. And every year, she sends us boxes of Christmas presents, wrapped in green and red. One year, I even sat on Santa's lap because that's what Grandma Taylor wanted for her present.

But I didn't know a thing about a Christmas tree. Real or fake.

◇

"Real always beats fake," I began. "Real butter beats margarine. Real sugar beats Splenda. A real singer beats a lip-syncher. So naturally, a real tree beats a fake one." I paused. "Because . . . it's real." I took a few steps, waiting for my brain to figure out where I was going. I'd had three minutes to prepare, but most of that time I'd spent frozen in shock.

"The Christmas season is about what's real. What is 'real' about our lives." I made quote marks with my fingers and took a few more steps. This was starting to feel okay. I went on. "Real family traditions. A real return to charity and goodwill. And what could be better than honoring these ideals with a real tree?

"Finally," I said, stretching out the word while I scrambled for a third point. "Finally, a real tree is simply much more beautiful. In fact," I said, picking up steam, "a real tree is so beautiful, it doesn't need decoration. Why have a real tree if you're going to put fake icicles on it, and fake shiny globes, and fake snowflakes? Because the next thing you know, you've got a real tree that looks fake. And people ask, is that tree real? And is it? Is it a real fake, or a fake real?"

A fake real? Had that really just come out of my mouth?

"In conclusion," I said quickly, "the natural choice is the fake one. I mean, the real one."

I looked at Mrs. Lee. I forced a smile. I wasn't sure, but it was possible that I'd just screwed that up.

"Thank you, Ellie," Mrs. Lee said. "I'm not sure how persuasive that was, but it was certainly entertaining."

I nodded, trying not to look as embarrassed as I suddenly felt. Megan once said I had an irrational fear of failure. But there was nothing irrational about it. Failure *sucked*.

I'd never been happier to head back to my seat. I was about to slide into it, when I caught a flash of red in the back of the room. I paused with my butt in midair and shot another look at the back corner—at a lady in a red blouse. She hadn't been there earlier. I would've noticed an older woman with silver hair and pale blue eyes. It couldn't be.

It couldn't be.

I twisted just enough to risk a quick look at Devon. Just in time to catch him exchanging a smile with the woman.

I squeezed the edges of my desk until my fingers ached. I leaned over to Sarah. "Who is that in the back of the room?"

"I've never met her," she whispered back. "But I think it's Doris Yeats."

I shut my eyes and groaned silently. "When did she come in? Did you see?" I opened my eyes, half afraid to hear the answer.

"She slipped in the back door a few minutes ago," Sarah said. "Right before you started."

CHAPTER 7

I set down my lunch tray next to Megan. "I am so screwed."

"Hello to you, too," she said. Then she tucked her blue-berry tie-dyed skirt under her legs and patted the bench.

I sunk down and took a long breath. Normally, I'd pause for a minute to marvel that the cafeteria air actually smelled decent. But today, the thought depressed me, along with the smooth tables that weren't carved up with graffiti, the floors that didn't stick with every step, and the cool overhead lights that hung down on invisible cables. I wanted a chance to eat lunch here every day. Thanks to my stupid impromptu, I might never get it.

It looked like I'd interrupted Megan in the middle of a slice of pepperoni and a gossip session with Anna. I could tell I was going to like Anna Hernandez, even though we'd just met yesterday at lunch.

Megan had sat next to Anna in their acting workshop, and they'd immediately bonded over a love of Ophelia and Juliet.

In other words, Anna also had a thing for Shakespeare's suicidal victims of love gone bad. She said she'd come to see a play at Benedict's when she was in fifth grade and knew instantly that life would not be worth living if she couldn't act on that stage. She put her name on the waiting list that same day, and still hadn't gotten in. Like me, she was holding out hope for a Benedict's Scholarship.

Anna had dark skin, wavy brown hair to her shoulders, and deep brown eyes. Today, she wore a white V-neck and khaki capris. A sack lunch spilled out in front of her, and she held a half-eaten Ding Dong in her hand. She had a pretty bad case of acne along her jawline, but a knockout smile. Which, at the moment, was covered in chocolate.

"So what happened?" Megan asked through a mouthful of crust.

"Mock impromptu." I stared at my lunch tray. Tiny pools of yellow grease had gathered on my cheese pizza.

"It tastes better if you don't look at it too long," Megan said, eyeing my pizza.

"And?" Anna urged.

I shoved the tray away. "My topic was Christmas trees."

"Isn't that an easy topic?" Anna asked.

"Not if you're Jewish," I said.

"You're Jewish?" Anna repeated. She'd moved on to her sandwich and gave me a peanut-butter-coated grin. "That's so cool—I love bagels and cream cheese."

"I bet you did fine." Megan grabbed a carrot off my plate. "You always come up with something."

41

"This time it was something hideously bad."

Anna laughed.

"It couldn't have been that bad," Megan insisted.

I twisted open a bottle of juice. "Remember your birthday when you turned seven and you wanted to give Island Princess Barbie a bath?" I asked. "And we decided to use the kitchen sink, but Barbie slipped down the drain? Remember how you went to turn on the light but accidentally turned on the disposal? Remember Barbie's legs when you fished her out?"

Megan nodded, trying not to laugh.

"That's how bad it was," I said. "And I haven't even told you the best part."

"It gets better?" Megan asked.

"There was a woman in the room. She must have come in the back door while I was turned away, preparing. She had silver hair and blue eyes."

Megan's smile crumbled into a startled *o*. "Mrs. Yeats was there?"

I nodded.

Even Anna looked worried now. "Uh-oh," she said under her breath.

My stomach did a 180. "What do you mean, uh-oh?"

Anna shrugged. "I've heard she can be tough. Some of the girls at registration were calling her Dynamite Doris—because she has a short fuse."

"Great." I groaned. "Just great."

Anna leaned in. "I heard she keeps a list of all the applicants for her scholarship. She looks for any reason to cross some-one off so she doesn't have to interview as many kids."

It was a good thing I hadn't eaten. I felt like throwing up. "So what do I do?"

"Just forget it," Megan said. "It's only day two of camp."

"It was just one class exercise," Anna seconded.

"The final tournament is what really counts," Megan added.

Everything they said was right, but right didn't matter. Winning did. I wound my fingers through my hair. "I've got to do something."

The cafeteria doors clanged open, and I looked up in time to see a pair of shoulders and a butt disappearing into the lobby. A nice set of shoulders. A nice butt.

Devon Yeats.

I straightened. If anyone could help, maybe . . . "I've got an idea."

"What idea?" Megan asked.

I grabbed my tray and stood up.

"Where are you going?"

"I talked my way into this mess," I said. "Maybe I can talk my way out of it."

Benedict's was laid out like a spider. The lobby, cafeteria, and auditorium were all in the center section of the school, and then eight hallways led off in different directions like legs. When I pushed open the cafeteria door, Devon had passed through the lobby and was heading down one of the legs on the right.

"Devon!" I called. He had his hand on a door. "Wait up." I hurried across the lobby, trying not to look like I was hurrying. "You got a minute?" I asked, a little breathless.

He gave me a funny look, then pointed at the door.

It was the boy's restroom. My face heated like a toaster. I backed away a couple of steps. "Right. No hurry. I'll be . . . uh . . . over here." I realized I was pointing my finger in the air like an idiot. I crossed my arms over my chest. "Just find me."

He grinned and disappeared inside.

I wanted to kick myself, but the way things were going, I'd lose my balance and fall over. I walked farther down the hall. There was a series of framed posters on the wall, all scenes from Shakespeare's plays. I pretended to read the one for *Romeo and Juliet* while I tried to slow my heart. A minute later, Devon caught up to me.

"What's up?" The sky blue color of his polo brought out his eyes—as if they needed bringing out.

I shook back my bangs and took a calming breath. At least, it was supposed to calm me. My heart was still thudding. It was hard enough to ask a favor when you knew the person. It was especially hard when the person in question was standing there looking bored and checking his watch. I forced a smile. "I wanted to talk to you about the exercise we did in class today."

He slid his hands in his pockets and nodded.

"I liked yours, by the way. Great intro—the whole paste thing."

"Thanks." He didn't return the compliment, I noticed, but he did smile wide enough for me to see that his teeth were white and straight. *Was anything about him* not *perfect?*

"So," I said. "This might sound weird, but I couldn't help noticing a woman in the back of the room."

He leaned against the wall. "My grandmother?"

"So it *was* your grandmother," I said, trying to sound like I hadn't been sure. "I heard she likes to catch the performances, but I didn't think that meant classroom exercises."

"She likes those, too." He nodded slowly, as if he'd figured out a puzzle. "You're one of *them*, aren't you?"

"That depends," I said, "on who 'them' are."

"One of the applicants for a Benedict's Scholarship."

I swallowed nervously. "Are there a lot of us?"

"More than you'd think." He pushed off the wall. "And I can't help you, if that's what you're hoping." He took a step toward the lobby like I was being dismissed.

I moved to cut off his path. I wasn't worried anymore. I was too annoyed to be worried. "I don't need help. Not exactly."

He eyed me suspiciously. "Then what?"

"I caught you exchanging looks when I finished. I just wondered if she said anything."

"About what?"

"About my performance."

His eyes narrowed. "She wouldn't say anything to me."

45

"But you exchanged that look."

"It was just a look."

"It didn't look like just a look." My voice was rising, but I couldn't help it. Did he have to make this so hard? "The thing is, I wasn't exactly sharp this morning, and I don't want her to get the wrong idea." A group of girls walked past. I glanced toward the lobby—it was starting to fill. Lunch must be almost over. I turned back to him. "Can you just tell her I was having an off-day?"

"How would I know that?" he said. "I only met you yesterday."

"I made sense yesterday."

"During our ice breaker, you spaced on the topic."

"I did not!"

His lips curved up. "Yeah, you did."

Arrogant jerk! And he wasn't all that good looking either, I decided, now that I saw him up close. He had a crease on his forehead—probably from looking down his nose all the time. "I still out-argued you."

"You didn't even know what you were arguing about."

"Which makes my performance even more impressive."

He started to say something, then stopped. His mouth hung open for a second. I couldn't tell if he wanted to laugh, or scream.

More kids worked their way down the hall; time was running out.

"I'm not asking you to lie," I said. "Just tell her I have potential."

His eyebrows dipped. "Unseen potential?"

I gasped as my nails dug into my palms. "I'm good enough to kick *your* butt."

He smiled. He actually smiled.

Which made my blood boil. "Fine. Wait until Friday. I'll prove it."

"Then you'll get your chance with my grandmother," he said.

I glared at his perfectly detestable face. "What does that mean?"

"It means there's one thing that always gets her attention." He flashed me a cocky half grin. "Beat her grandson. If you can."

CHAPTER 8

"Can you believe he said that?" I waited for Zeydeh to look as mad as I still felt.

I'd spent the night at Megan's and fumed about it for hours with her. Megan said it was obvious that Devon needed a good butt-kicking, and I was just the person to give it to him. I hadn't had a chance to tell Zeydeh the whole story, so I'd gotten up early for Juice Duty. I figured I could tell him every detail before it was time for camp. I didn't count on his putting me to work.

"Careful," Zeydeh ordered, looking over my shoulder. "Scoop gently."

The early morning sun slanted through Zeydeh's kitchen window, turning the batter a pale yellow.

Zeydeh lived five houses down from us in the smallest home on our street. It was tucked back—almost like an afterthought. When it came on the market after Bubbe died,

Zeydeh said it was perfect—he didn't want to get in anyone's way. Mom laughed at that. She said Zeydeh's greatest pleasure was getting in *everyone's* way.

I sighed and slid my fingers into the mixture of matzo meal, eggs, salt, pepper, and Zeydeh's seasonings. I cupped a palm full of the batter and rounded it into a lumpy circle. When the matzo balls cooked up, they would be light and fluffy—like melt-in-your-mouth dumplings. But right now, the batter was gooey and stuck to my palms.

"It's not a baseball in your hands," Zeydeh snapped. "And if you're not gentle, it'll taste like one." He gestured for me to keep working. "So, this Devon Yeats sounds very sure of himself."

"It's because of that stupid topic yesterday. I still can't believe it. Everyone else gets books or movies, and I get Christmas trees."

"I told you this camp was not for you."

"It's just bad luck." I dropped a sticky ball into the pot of soup. "Explain to me again why you're cooking matzo balls at eight in the morning?" I held up my hands, coated in batter. "Make that, why am *I* cooking matzo balls at eight in the morning?"

"It's only three weeks until the contest—I have no time to waste. If I could roll the batter myself, I would, but you know my arthritis is bad in the mornings."

I sighed and dug back in. "Why did Mrs. Yeats have to pick that minute to stop in our room?" I paused, suddenly noticing Zeydeh's orange juice on the counter. It had separated so the top half was a lighter orange than the bottom. "Zeydeh, you didn't drink your juice!"

He rolled his eyes. "Always with the juice." He reached for the glass and took two swallows, swishing it around his mouth like mouthwash. "There, happy?"

Then he squinted down at my hands. "Smaller, Ellie." He wagged a finger. "That's the secret. Smaller balls in bigger pots. You mark my words: they'll fluff up like your Bubbe's hair in a windstorm." Suddenly, he leaned forward and looked out the window.

"What?" I asked.

"I caught Mrs. Zuckerman spying on me yesterday. I wouldn't be surprised if she's skulking in the bushes."

I dropped another ball into the soup. "You think she's spying?"

"I don't *think*. I *know*." He went into squint mode. "I caught her walking by the house this morning, as if she likes to take morning walks."

"Zeydeh," I said, "she *does* like to take morning walks."

Mrs. Zuckerman lived across the street at the end of the block. She used to walk with her husband every afternoon. After he died, she shifted to mornings. I saw her all the time on my way for Juice Duty. Like Zeydeh, Mrs. Zuckerman also entered the Har Zion Cooking Contest every year. But unlike Zeydeh, Mrs. Zuckerman won the Har Zion Cooking Contest every year.

"*Hoomf*," he muttered. "It's a cover. She's sniffing around to see what I'm cooking. She knows, Ellie. She knows this year it'll be Samuel Levine's name on the plaque."

"Just don't let your blood pressure get out of whack," I warned.

"Don't worry about me," he said, shrugging. "Either I win or I die trying."

I stopped rolling the batter. "Is that supposed to be comforting?"

"Quit worrying and keep rolling," he retorted. "You're the one whose blood pressure is off the charts today."

I squeezed a hunk of batter, feeling it squish out between my fingers. "Devon Yeats is going to eat his words."

"And what is the speech about for Friday?"

"I don't know," I said. "Mrs. Lee will tell us today."

"Whatever it is, I'll be there to watch. You've been wearing Bubbe's necklace?"

I shook my head. "I don't want to lose it."

"You won't lose it," he said. "Wear it. It'll bring you good luck."

I rolled a finger around the tip of the mixing bowl, dropping spatters of mix back to the bottom. "I could use some luck after the whole Christmas tree disaster."

"Enough already," Zeydeh snapped. "I'm tired of hearing it."

I blinked up at him, startled. Zeydeh never snapped at me. He never got mad at me for real. But now his jaw was sticking out and his eyes were glaring.

"If it was so important, you would have opened your mouth."

"What do you mean?" I said. "I did open my mouth. Just nothing good came out."

"I'm not referring to the words that came out of your mouth. I'm referring to the words that did *not*."

I stared. "What are you talking about?"

"You could have asked for another topic. Explained why you wanted one."

"I would have looked like a whiner."

"No," he said, pointing a finger at me. "You would have looked like a Jew."

I gasped. "That doesn't have anything to do with it."

"Doesn't it?" he retorted. "It seems to me you had a choice. Look like a Jew, or look like an idiot. You chose to look like an idiot."

"I didn't choose anything!"

"We all choose, Ellie," he said. "Sometimes by not choosing at all."

CHAPTER 9

"Since it's Wednesday, you may be wondering about Friday's speech," Mrs. Lee began. This morning she'd lectured on research. We had to cite seven to ten sources in our final oratories, plus keep note cards on how each resource related to our topic. It was pretty dry stuff, but now my heart sped up.

"Imagine," she said, "you've gathered for the funeral of a pet. This could be a most beloved pet of yours. This could be the evil cat next door or a little green ferret from Mars who lives only in your mind. It can be any pet you imagine, but you are the one giving the eulogy—the speech commemorating the life of this pet. Your eulogy must be between three and five minutes. I'll be judging on six criteria," she added.

I took notes as she listed them off, but half my brain was already thinking up the perfect pet. Talk about potential. I just needed something cool. Something that would stand out.

She checked the clock. "You have twenty minutes before

lunch. By the time the bell rings, I'd like a piece of paper on my desk with your name and the pet you plan to eulogize. Questions?" She scanned the room, and then nodded. "Get busy."

I pulled out a clean sheet of paper. I wrote "Eulogy" at the top. Then I left my pen poised over the paper. The trick to brainstorming was to write whatever came to your mind, and eventually something good would come. So I started writing.

cats dogs lizards hamsters gerbils pigs
piggy banks—cracked open a piggy bank?
mules moles monkeys—chimp—
    Curious George ????
fantasy pet—teacher's pet

I tapped my pen on the paper. A splinter of worry stabbed deep in my stomach. Nothing seemed right. Nancy, Kim, and Peter had already turned in their papers. My ears felt hypersensitive, waiting to pick up the sounds of the next person walking to Mrs. Lee's desk. I bent over my paper and started again.

fish? eulogy over a toilet?
frog—Prince Charming
parrot—singing parrot—American-Idol-
    winning parrot

Sarah, Ethan, and Andrew handed in their sheets. Was I the only one drawing a blank? My pen tapped faster, keeping pace with my thudding heart.

Devon walked by next, in his perfectly pressed gray shorts and white polo. He looked fresh out of a movie poster. I felt a little sticky under my arms, and the back of my neck was hot. His paper flapped in the air. I leaned forward without meaning to, and caught myself squinting to read his writing. I couldn't make out a word of it, and I sat back, mad at myself for even looking.

Concentrate.

I felt him glance at me as he passed my desk. I covered my notes as if there was something worth covering. As soon as he went back to his desk, I scanned my scribbles again.

Nothing!

I glanced at the clock. Less than ten minutes before lunch.

I wadded up the sheet and tossed it at the trash can. It hit the rim, and fell to the carpet. *Figures.* I slid out of my seat, reached the paper, and dropped it into the barrel.

And froze.

The trashcan wasn't empty. There was a white plastic liner inside, and at the bottom were four sheets of paper wadded up, some ripped index cards, an empty water bottle—and a snack-size box of cereal. Colors and images flashed up at me. Chocolate brown, orange feathers, and a yellow beak. A seriously huge, yellow beak.

That beak was my break!

I walked back to my desk, but inside I was skipping. Inside, I was turning cartwheels and high-fiving my fabulous self. I pulled out a clean sheet of paper and wrote, "Sonny, The Cocoa

Puffs Cuckoo Bird." Six little words. They'd be enough to put me back in the running.

Proudly, I handed the paper to Mrs. Lee. She blinked, then looked up at me.

I expected a smile—maybe even a glimmer of approval in her eyes. Instead, she frowned. Her green eyes narrowed.

I reached for Bubbe's necklace, my good-luck charm. I ran a finger around the chain. "What?"

She cleared her throat. "Could I see you outside in the hall for a minute?"

I swallowed and looked at my paper, my heart stuttering a little. She'd said any pet I wanted. "Yeah, sure."

She flipped through the other sheets of paper and pulled one out. "Devon," she said. "Would you join us in the hall?"

I didn't know what to think—which was good since my brain had frozen with panic. Mrs. Lee was only a little taller than me, but I felt two inches high as she led the way into the hall, and then closed the door behind us.

She held a sheet of paper in each hand. "I have two papers with the exact same pet."

Devon and I swapped surprised looks.

"The odds of this happening are only slightly better than my winning the lottery. And I never win the lottery." She looked mad. "I simply have to ask the question: How did you both choose your pet?" She looked at me. "Ellie?"

"There was a Cocoa Puffs box in the trash." I gestured toward the room. "You can take a look, if you want. As soon as I saw it, I got the idea."

Devon shot me a look. "That was my box. I ate the cereal on the way to camp this morning."

Mrs. Lee let out a long breath. "Thank goodness." She handed back our papers. "I didn't want to escort one of you out for cheating. So," she added, "we know how it happened. The question now is what would you like to do about it?"

Devon fluttered his paper. "Why do we have to do anything?"

"We can't both do the same pet," I said.

"Why not?"

"We won't be unique." *Duh.* And, I added to myself, *Jerk!*

"Yeah, we will."

I rolled my eyes. *Could he possibly be any more annoying?* I looked at Mrs. Lee. "I think it's a bad idea."

"Fine," Devon said with an easy shrug. "Then pick another pet."

I raised my eyebrows. "Why should *I* pick another pet?"

"Because you're the one who cares."

It was confirmed. He could be more annoying.

Mrs. Lee sighed. "Nothing's easy with speech students, is it? You have until the bell rings, and then I need your decision." She slipped back into the room.

I glared at his paper. He wrote like a guy—blocky and messy—but the words were still clear: "Coocoo Bird." I narrowed my eyes and stared harder. "That's not how you spell 'cuckoo.'"

He glanced at his paper. "So?"

"So why should you get the pet if you can't even spell it?"

57

◇◇◇◇◇

"Who cares about spelling?"

"If you liked cuckoo birds, you'd know how to spell the word."

"I don't like cuckoo birds," he retorted. "I like little round cereals with lots of chocolate and sugar. And I like saying 'cuckoo,'" he added.

"That's why you chose it? So you can say 'cuckoo' in front of an audience?"

He slid his hands in his pockets like Mr. Too-Cool-for-Words. "You got a better reason?"

"Yeah," I snapped. "I chose it because it's a perfect way to beat you."

He rolled his eyes. "You're not going to beat me."

"Not if you do the same pet."

"I picked the pet first. You were going to do Curious George."

I gasped, my cheeks suddenly burning. "You looked at my notes?"

"How could I miss it? I mean, Curious George?"

"He happens to be a very cool monkey."

I shot him a glare, and he surprised me by grinning. There was a challenge in his eyes, but also laughter. He was enjoying this.

"I'm *soooo* glad you find this funny."

"Well, we have to do something." He checked his watch. "What do you think? Rock, paper, scissors?"

"Rock, paper, scissors? Are you crazy?"

"If you're afraid to go head-to-head—"

"Who said I was afraid?" I interrupted. I lifted my chin

again, wishing I were taller so I didn't have to look up. "I thought it would be better to have different pets, but if you don't mind, then I don't mind."

"You don't?"

"I can beat you either way."

He was smiling again. "You think so, huh?"

"I know so."

His eyes glinted at me, dark and light—hot and cold—all at the same time. "We'll find out on Friday," he said. He held out his hand. "May the best dead cuckoo win."

It was a dare—a bet—and I took his hand to seal the deal. A quick, firm handshake to show him I meant business.

And then it happened.

A jolt.

An electric shiver. From his hand to mine.

It was like seventh-grade science class. The day we mixed baking soda and vinegar. And two things that were calm suddenly sizzled.

I sizzled.

◇

"Describe the sizzle—exactly!" Megan demanded.

Dad had dropped us off after camp at the corner store for ice cream cones. Megan had a double scoop of pralines and cream. I got a triple of brownie fudge. If anything could settle my churning stomach, it was chocolate.

"It wasn't really a sizzle," I said, heading for the crosswalk.

She crunched a praline in her teeth. "You said sizzle."

I never should have used the word "sizzle" with Megan. "It was sizzlelike. Okay? As in, approaching sizzle." I picked a brownie off the top of my cone and ate it. "It was just competitive fire—you know, from the challenge."

She gave me her death stare. "Just describe it."

I waited for a car to pass, and then we crossed the street. "I don't know. Like a shiver, only bad."

"That's not competitive fire, Ellie. That's love."

"You think everything is love."

"That's because I'm an optimist," she said, flashing a sticky smile.

"It can't be," I said. "How can I sizzle for a guy *and* want to kick his butt? I don't even *like* him. He's arrogant, he acts like he knows everything, and you can tell he's used to getting whatever he wants."

"And," Megan added, "he's smart, and funny, and you know you have a shallow thing for model-boy good looks."

"Ninety-nine point nine percent of the population does, too."

"Can I help it if I'm more highly evolved?" She dug back in to her ice cream, and so did I. As we walked, my tower of scoops turned into a small hill. Megan was down to the cone.

"So did Anna get a letter from Yeats?" I finally asked.

Megan pretended to chase after a drip of ice cream, but I saw the flinch of her shoulders, which meant she'd just tensed. Which meant that yes, Anna had gotten a letter.

Just like that, it felt like I had a brick of brownies in my stomach. "When did she get it?"

"This afternoon."

"Megan!" My stomach churned again—not even chocolate could help me now. I tossed my cone as we passed an alley.

"It doesn't mean anything," she said.

"Yeah, it does," I muttered. "It means everything." It meant Doris Yeats had sent out letters to set up interviews. And I hadn't gotten one.

"She doesn't interview everyone," Megan added. "That's what it said on the application, right? Only if she has follow-up questions."

"That's just to make complete losers feel better when they don't get a letter." We crossed to my street. My house was the third one down where the sidewalk showed a patch of shade from our ficus tree. "She only sends out letters to the ones she's serious about. I'm already off the list. Game over."

"Just until you do your eulogy." We reached the shade of the tree and Megan paused. "You're going to get up on that stage and blow Devon out of the cuckoo water."

The branches of the ficus tree hung down over me like the fingers of a giant hand. I stood in the tiny bit of cool, imagining that it was God's hand spread over my head. Every week on the Jewish Sabbath, there's a special prayer parents say for each child. But in our house, it was always Zeydeh who would rest his hand over my head and ask for God's blessing. I thought of that now, standing under the protective branches that trembled just a little—just like Zeydeh's hand.

"I have to beat him, Megan," I whispered. "I have to."

Even to me, it sounded like a little prayer.

CHAPTER 10

"Some said Sonny was a strange bird," I began solemnly. "But Sonny was just a little cuckoo." I paused and held up a box of cereal. "He was the Cocoa Puffs Cuckoo Bird."

I stood center stage, looking at the small audience in the auditorium. Dad, Zeydeh, and Benny sat in the third row. There were other families, too—enough to fill the center seats of four rows. The Big Three sat in the front: Mrs. Lee, my judge; Mrs. Clancy, my timekeeper; Mrs. Doris Yeats, my future.

People said you could feed off laughter and it was true. Standing up there, I felt like a human Pac-Man—swallowing up bites of laughter and growing stronger. I could hear Zeydeh's laugh—a low rumble that always sounded on the verge of exploding into a cough but never did. And Dad. He'd heard the eulogy so many times he could probably recite it, but he still laughed like the first time. The rest of the audience was laughing, too.

I kept my face straight and blinked dramatically, pretending to dab at a tear with a white lace hanky I'd borrowed from Mom. I wore black pants and a black shirt just to set the mood.

"Sonny struggled to live a normal life. He tried low-carb diets, hypnosis, and years of therapy. But in the end, he always gave in to his love for the puffs of cocoa."

I paused to breathe in more laughter and launched into the details of Sonny's life. The words flowed as I moved across stage—I was totally in the zone. I dabbed a last time at my eye, then said, "One taste of the munchy, crunchy chocolaty puffs sent Sonny flying high. Until one day, he flew just a little too close to the ceiling fan. Now, just like Sonny"—another pause—"mourners everywhere are falling to pieces."

There was a burst of groans and laughter, then applause. I smiled and bowed to the front row, careful to make eye contact, then walked down the steps and took my seat next to Sarah.

"Nice," she whispered.

"Thanks." I tried not to beam. *Mrs. Yeats had been smiling— definitely smiling!* Andrew Sawyer was halfway through his ode to Odie—a pet goldfish—before I felt the ground under my feet again.

Then Andrew took his seat and Devon climbed the stairs. He wore a suit—coat, tie, the whole works. I had a sudden image of Devon in a tuxedo. Cooler than cool—but hot. Like James Bond before he got old. Devon's level of "hotness" was a daily afternoon-break topic with the other girls in class. I never said anything. I couldn't exactly deny it. Still, I secretly hoped he'd show up today with a huge zit on his chin. Did guys like Devon ever get zits?

"Flighty at times, but with a heart as big as his beak. That was our cuckoo." Devon launched into his eulogy with a seriousness that should have made me gag. But he pulled off the whole sensitive-guy thing. When he finished, I had to admit he was good.

I just didn't have to admit it to him.

I stood to let him slide in past me.

"A standing ovation?" he said, pretending to look flattered.

"You were good," I muttered. "But not that good."

He grinned.

I rolled my eyes. He couldn't even take an insult the right way. I made myself as skinny as possible so he could pass with no contact, but my face still felt warm for some stupid reason.

Twenty minutes later, everyone had presented and Mrs. Lee had tallied up all our scores. She stood at the edge of the stage, a notepad in her hands. "First of all," she said, "nice job, everyone. And thank you, family and friends. It always adds an element of reality to have an audience." She looked down at her pad. "I'll have in-depth notes for each of you, but for now, I'm pleased to announce our top three. In third, Sarah McCloud."

I shot Sarah a big smile and a thumbs-up. Then I sat forward and crossed my fingers.

"Second place, Ellie Taylor."

Oh God! It was like someone had taken wet fingers and pinched out the flicker of hope inside me. *Zzipt.* Gone. Dark. I plastered on a fake smile, but I had to close my eyes against what I knew was coming next.

"And the winner," Mrs. Lee said, "is Devon Yeats."

That was that. My shoulders slumped in defeat. Not only had I lost, but I'd lost to *Devon*. It was only the first week of camp, but it might as well be over. I might as well write another eulogy. For me.

CHAPTER 11

Got lost zinken, ober nit dertrinken: God lets you sink but not drown.

It was one of Zeydeh's favorite Yiddish expressions—and he had a million of them. It kept running through my head—but only the first part. God lets you sink.

I'd said good-bye to Dad, Zeydeh, and Benny a few minutes ago, then snuck off to lick my wounds in private. I'd wandered down one of the spider-leg halls and discovered a window nook in a tiny alcove. Beneath shaded windows, a seat bench ran in a semicircle, topped with a thick red cushion.

I kicked off my sandals and rested my head on the wall. Just how far did God let you sink? I'd have to ask Zeydeh. It was one of those details I'd never worried about before.

I let loose a breath—and along with it, my brave face. I pulled up my knees and hugged them to my chest. *You got a minute, God? Because I could really use some help here.* I looked up toward the ceiling. *I hate to always bother you with my problems, and I know I ask too many favors, but for me, this is big. And I'm really looking out for your interests here, too. After all, you created me in your image, which means you must also love to talk. And it's no good to talk if no one hears you, and how can I be heard—really heard in this world—if I don't get this scholarship? Which is why a miracle would really come in handy right now.*

"Ellie?"

I shrieked and jumped halfway out of my skin. Devon stood a few feet away. *Perfect—I ask for a miracle and get a nightmare.*

"You scared me," I said. I laid a hand over my chest. My heart slammed against my ribs.

"Sorry." He'd taken off his suit coat, and his tie hung loose around his collar.

When he didn't move, I asked, "Is it time for class or something?"

He shook his head. "Mind if I sit?"

I squinted my eyes in a classic Zeydeh stare. "Yeah, I mind. You can gloat standing up."

"I only gloat in front of a crowd."

Then he gave me this sincere, nice-guy smile, so even though a part of me wanted to kick him, I had to move to let him sit.

I slid my feet back into my sandals. For some reason, my stupid heart started hammering again. It was his smile, I decided. A nice smile like that had to mean he was up to something. Devon wasn't suddenly going to turn into a decent guy. At least I hoped not. I planned to hate him forever.

He sat down across from me. His hands tapped the side of the bench as he looked around. "This is cool."

I waited. *What did he want?*

"Nice job today," he said.

"If that's gloating, it's pretty weak."

He ran a hand through his hair, spiking up the edges around his ear. In this light, his hair looked almost blue black. "The ceiling-fan thing was really funny."

"Not funny enough, apparently." I felt the hard edge of the star bite into my fingers, and realized I was fiddling with my necklace. I crossed my arms over my stomach.

"So why are you hiding out?"

"Who said I was hiding out?"

"Do you argue about everything?"

"No."

"That's arguing."

"Define arguing."

He grinned and relaxed back against the wall. "Everyone was wondering where you went. Andrew and Ethan are still laughing about falling to pieces."

"Too bad they weren't judging," I said. But I couldn't help it—I felt myself thawing a little. "So what happened to you doing something funny with the cuckoo?"

"I tried," he said. "I'm not good with humor."

"Your impromptu on Monday was funny."

"Yeah, but that was off the cuff. It just came out. As soon as I start writing, I turn into Mr. Term Paper."

"I wouldn't complain," I said. "You were good."

"Good but boring. It'd be cool to really make people laugh."

"Only if you're trying to be funny," I said, dryly. "Otherwise, it kind of sucks."

He laughed—a short burst that took me by surprise. Come to think of it, the whole thing was surprising. Me, sitting here with Devon Yeats.

"What?" he said. "You just got a weird look on your face."

"I can't believe I'm talking with the enemy."

"Me?"

"In case you missed it, you won. I lost."

He draped an arm over one knee. "It was just an exercise."

"It wasn't just an exercise. Your grandmother was there, remember? Dynamite Doris."

"Dynamite Doris?" he repeated. "Is that because she's such a blast?"

I covered my face with a hand and groaned. "I can't believe I just called her that."

"I won't tell."

I snuck a look from under my fingers. "You're not going to turn into a nice guy, are you? Because I was getting used to despising you."

He laughed again. It felt good hearing his laugh. Which was amazing, I realized, because I hadn't planned to feel good for at least a month.

"So why is she called Dynamite Doris?" Devon asked.

"She's got a rep for making quick decisions." My smile collapsed as I thought about the scholarship. "Deadly decisions for some of us."

"The scholarship, you mean?"

"That's the whole reason I signed up for this camp."

"So?"

"So," I said sharply, "you told me the only way to get her attention was to beat you."

"What's with the necklace?" he asked, his gaze dropping below my chin.

I looked down, and realized I was twirling the Jewish star again. "My grandpa gave it to me to wear. It was my grandma's."

"You're Jewish?"

I nodded, fingering the star. "You sound surprised."

He shrugged. "You're at a Christian camp. And your name— Taylor's not a Jewish name, is it?"

"My dad isn't Jewish," I said. "He was raised Lutheran."

"Ohhhh." He nodded. "So that's cool."

I frowned, the muscles around my shoulders tensing. "What's cool?"

"Being half and half," he said. "You get double presents in December, right?"

I had to smile—how many times had I heard that? "I get the same number of presents, just different colors of wrapping paper." I straightened the necklace chain where it had gotten caught in my hair. "My grandpa says you can't be half of anything."

"The grandpa who gave you the necklace?"

I nodded. "It's supposed to be good luck, but it didn't quite work that way."

"Maybe it did."

"I had to win today to get back on her list."

"What list?"

"Letters went out, Devon. I didn't get one. If she's considering you, you get a letter. If you get a letter, you get an interview. She only interviews the top candidates, no matter what it says on the application. No letter, no interview, no chance."

"Except," he said, raising his eyebrows a half inch, "if you have no chance, why does she want to meet you?"

I froze in midbreath. "What?"

He grinned. "She wants to meet you."

I stared into his eyes, looking for the truth. The truth was that he had gorgeous eyes. "She said that? She wants to meet me? Why didn't you tell me right off?" I kicked his shoe with my sandal. His grin widened. I wasn't sure if it was his words or the way he was smiling at me, but my arms prickled with goose bumps.

"That's not all she said."

My eyes probably looked the size of planets, but I didn't care. "What?"

"Just that you have an expressive style. And, she thought you should have won."

"Yes!" I said, pumping a fist. "I'm back in!"

He laughed. "You really want this, huh?"

"You have no idea." I paused for a silent scream of happiness. Then I slid to the edge of the bench. "So when does she want to meet?"

"Now."

My heart stuttered. "Now?"

"That's why I was looking for you."

I gripped the edge of the cushion. "Now?"

"Unless now is bad."

I swallowed. "No. Now is good." I stood up.

He stood, too. "You okay?"

"Yeah." I took a deep breath. "It's just so quick. After I lost, well . . . I always say you can argue your way into anything. I guess I'd started to think I couldn't argue my way into Benedict's."

"If anyone can, you can."

I'd seen Devon smile politely at Mrs. Lee. I'd seen him smile with other kids during lunch. I'd seen him smile on stage. But there was something about this smile. Something so warm . . . I felt like a chocolate bar left on the dashboard. If he kept smiling like that, I'd melt into a gooey mess. I didn't want to know what Megan would make of that.

"Come on," he said. "I'll walk you to Admin. My grand-mother bought the speech department all new computers and printers, so they gave her the vice principal's office for the summer. She's supposed to be here supervising the install and interviewing kids, but mostly I think she likes dropping in on the classes."

I followed him down the hall, smoothing my hair. "So what do I say?"

"Just tell her how impressive Benedict's is. She loves that stuff. And—" He paused. His feet trickled to a stop, the way his words had.

"What?" I stopped beside him, straightening my shirt. "Is something wrong?"

"Not wrong, exactly." He ran a hand through his hair again. "It's just your necklace. You might want to stick it inside your shirt."

I fingered the warm metal. "Why?"

"It's not a big deal." His eyes shifted toward Admin. "She's just a little weird about the Jewish thing."

"Huh?" The *Jewish thing*? I made myself take a breath. *Weird?* What did that mean? It couldn't really mean what it sounded like, could it? I stood there a second, off balance. My brain off balance.

"It's not a big deal. Really."

"Oh-kay." *Not a big deal.* I couldn't process anything else beyond the fact that her office was just up ahead, and Devon had started walking slowly in that direction. I took a few small steps while my mind raced. Maybe I should just get through this first meeting, and then I could ask Devon what he meant. For now, I should focus on Benedict's. On my expressive style. On my future.

So many thoughts swirled through my brain I wasn't sure if I nodded or not.

But I slid the necklace inside my shirt.

CHAPTER 12

Doris Yeats sat behind a heavy oak desk, one hand wrapped around a cup of coffee, the other scrawling something with a fancy red fountain pen.

Devon knocked on the open door and she glanced up. I wasn't sure what I was expecting—a swastika tattoo on her forehead? She looked like a normal grandmother. Short silver hair like a cap over a small face with high cheekbones and a wide mouth. When she saw who it was, her whole face seemed to soften. Her eyes were the same startling blue as Devon's, only a little faded. She stood and walked around the desk, looking very stylish in a cream suit and smelling expensive.

"How nice of you to come." She smiled and lines fanned out from the corners of her eyes and mouth. The edge of one front tooth had a teeny tiny chip. I wanted to like her.

"Ellie, this is my grandmother, Doris Yeats," Devon said.

"Nice to meet you," I said.

She held out her hand. She was the same height as me, but tiny—even her fingers looked small. But her grip was strong, as if she had wire running through her. Her skin felt soft and smooth, not papery like Zeydeh's.

"Shall we sit for a minute?" she asked. She gave Devon a warm smile. "Not you. You've done your good deed, now get to class."

"Yes, Grandmother," he said in a fake obedient voice. Then he grinned my way. "I'll let Mrs. Lee know you'll be late."

I nodded, telling him thanks with my eyes.

Doris Yeats watched him go, obviously proud. "He did a marvelous eulogy today, though I don't think he deserved first place."

She gestured to the cream love seat set against the wall.

I carefully sat on one edge. Mrs. Yeats sat next to me, crossing her legs and folding her hands over her covered knees. I tried to copy the pose without looking like it.

"I imagine Devon told you I was impressed with your performance."

"He did," I admitted, then added, "I was really hoping you would be."

She laughed lightly, her high cheekbones becoming more pronounced. "I have to say, after hearing your speech in class, I wondered if you had the skill for real humor. Too often content is lost in the quest for easy laughs. However, you did an admirable job today."

"Thank you."

"Humor in oratories continues to be successful in

competition. As sponsor of the Benedict's speech team, I'm always on the lookout for students with talent in that area."

I twisted my fingers together, trying to look intense but not desperate. "I would love the opportunity to go to Benedict's. I would work so hard, and with the coaching here, I could do amazing things."

She smiled. "Benedict's is a very special school, which is why so many students must be turned away each year. I'm privileged to have the opportunity and the means to provide one or two scholarships each year to students with both need and talent."

I nodded as she went on. Her expression had turned very serious. "Benedict's isn't just a school to me, Ellie, it's my extended family. My husband was a Benedict's graduate, as was Devon's father, and now Devon will be continuing the tradition. The school has given so much to my family; I feel honored to give something back."

"Devon told me about the new computers you're donating." *Please, please, let me be one of the kids who gets to use them.*

"I try to do as much as I can. That includes helping to ensure that each new student fits in with our family. You understand?"

"Of course."

She smiled as if I'd said all the right things. "Then you won't mind filling out a questionnaire I have for scholarship applicants. I find it's helpful for the interview process." Then she stood. "If you'd fill it out, please, then have your parents sign the bottom."

She went back to her desk, rummaged through a stack of papers, and pulled out a white folder. "You may return it on Monday, and we'll schedule an interview for, say . . ." She slipped on a pair of glasses and looked at her calendar. "Next Friday?"

I hugged the folder to my chest and nodded. "Thank you, Mrs. Yeats."

And thank you, God!

I floated my way toward class. Talk about a miracle.

I got an interview!

I flipped open the folder and took a quick look at the questionnaire. The front side had the usual questions about my previous experience and any awards or top finishes. There were questions about goals, areas to improve, and what I could bring to the speech team. I flipped it over. The back was mostly personal information—contact numbers, family members and—*oh no.* I stopped and tried to hold the paper steady, but my fingers were shaking. Still, it was clear enough to read:

#7: What is your religious affiliation?

I reached for my necklace, but it was still under my shirt. Where I'd hidden it.

She's a little weird about the Jewish thing.

Devon's words flashed through my mind. I'd forgotten all about that. I traced the outline of the star with my fingers. Slipping a necklace inside my shirt was one thing. But she'd see it on the application. There was no way around that.

Beneath the Star of David, my heart shivered.

CHAPTER 13

Megan glanced over the questionnaire, then handed it back to me. "It doesn't *look* complicated."

"Believe me," I said in a low voice, "it's complicated. I still haven't told you everything."

I lay back on her bed and breathed in the wisteria scent that Hannah sprayed every day. Hannah was the cleaning lady, and I never saw her without a can of air freshener. Not that anything in the Swan house ever smelled. Megan had no pets and no brothers—which eliminated 99 percent of all odors. And she was the only one in the house who ever farted. Her parents would die first.

I still wore my black clothes from camp. I'd sweated through the top, but I didn't want to take time to go home and change. I had to figure out what to do, and Megan had to help. I couldn't talk to her with my dad in the car, but I'd warned Megan to prepare for something big.

By the time we'd grabbed Dr Peppers from the fridge and Double Stufs from the pantry, I'd told her about the eulogies—about my second place, and slinking off to the window nook to hide. While we circled the dining room, walked through the study and behind the home theater, I told her about Devon's finding me. As we climbed the winding staircase to Megan's bedroom, I told her about the meeting with Mrs. Yeats.

And after she kicked off her orange Crocs and dropped into a beanbag chair, I showed her the questionnaire.

Now, I had to tell her the rest. I sat up, grabbed a pink, fluffy pillow from the back of her bed, and wrapped my arms around it. "Here's the kicker. Devon told me to hide my Jewish star before I met his grandmother. Apparently, Dynamite Doris has a weird thing about Jews."

Megan pushed her glasses up on her nose. "No way!"

"Exactly," I muttered. "And now I have to fill out a questionnaire that says I'm Jewish."

"Oh-kay," she said slowly. "That *is* a little complicated."

I shifted on the thick mattress. Megan's room was so not Megan. It was like someone had barfed cotton candy all over everything. Mrs. Swan had seen a picture of it in a luxury-homes magazine and called in the decorator. The house was a showpiece, and that included Megan's room.

Megan said her mother did it just to piss her off. Megan liked to say they have a love-hate relationship: they love to hate each other. According to Megan, Mrs. Swan can't stand the horror of having given birth to an ugly duckling. (Megan has fought off all attempts to be a "swan" in anything but name.) And according to Mrs. Swan, Megan acts out just to be rebellious.

I think they're both right.

I dug my toes into her pink puffy comforter. "I don't know what to do." I stared at the questionnaire where it lay on the bed. A rectangle of white on a pink background. "What do you think?"

Megan shook up a bottle of black nail polish. It sounded like a mini–pinball machine as it mixed. "First of all, you should talk to Devon. Find out what he means. Doris is weird in what way?"

"Is there a good way?"

She thought for a second. "Maybe she once got food poisoning from a bad piece of lox, and the word 'Jewish' still gives her the runs."

I groaned. "Nice mental picture, thanks."

She laughed and opened the bottle. The wisteria faded under the sharp scent of polish as Megan spread the black over her thumbnail. "I'm just saying it doesn't have to be something awful like anti-Semitism. I mean, that's so last century, isn't it? And this is America. The Home of the Free and the Semi-intelligent."

"Devon did start off by saying it wasn't a big deal. But if it's not a big deal, why tell me to hide the necklace?"

"That's why you have to ask."

"That should go over real well." I tried to imagine it. "Uh, by the way, Devon, is your grandmother a Nazi?" I looked at Megan to see if that sounded as bad to her as it had to me.

She nodded. "I see the problem."

"Besides, I met Mrs. Yeats. She was really nice." I rested my chin on the pillow. "If only it wasn't on the questionnaire. It wouldn't ever have to come up."

Megan nodded. "Problems are so much easier to deal with when you can ignore them."

"I can't lie," I said.

"Depends on what you mean by lying." Megan switched the bottle and started on her other hand. "What you've got to do is look at it like an interview for a job. You want the job of going to Benedict's, right? Which makes this questionnaire a job application."

"That makes sense."

"So you want to give yourself the best chance." She waved the polish brush at me. "Accentuate the positive. Tell them what they want to hear. That's not lying. That's good business sense."

"In other words, say I'm Christian?"

"If that's what she wants to hear."

"But it's a lie."

"Not technically," Megan said. "Your dad is Lutheran."

"Yeah, but he doesn't act like it. We don't go to church, and unless Grandma and Grandpa Taylor are around, we don't do Christian holidays. I couldn't even do an impromptu on a Christmas tree."

"Doesn't matter. It's still in your dad's blood, which means it's in your blood."

"That works?"

"It worked for Hitler. He killed people for being one-eighth Jewish. If it can work against you, why can't it work for you?"

"Oh God," I said, suddenly remembering. I looked at the bottom of the form. "My parents have to sign this."

Megan paused. "Will they?"

"If I say I'm a Christian?" I thought a minute. "Well, maybe. They don't make a big deal about religion—not like Zeydeh."

"You can *not* let your zeydeh see this!" Megan breathed.

I shuddered, just imagining it. "He'd freak."

"And then he'd let loose some seriously good swear words."

Megan loved Yiddish swear words. She could call a kid a *szhlob* and he'd never know he'd just been called a moron. Megan also loved Zeydeh—almost as much as I did. According to Megan, it was a black-and-white world but Zeydeh had color.

I read the question about religious affiliation again. "Why does she even care?"

Megan blew on her nails. "She probably wants kids just like her. Rich people are all into conformity."

"I'll be a good orator no matter what religion I am. Isn't that what matters?"

"Obviously."

"And Devon's the one who told me to hide my necklace. He's her grandson—he wouldn't have said anything if the reason was really bad."

"Unless he likes you."

"He doesn't like me like that."

"He thinks you're funny."

"Maybe he thinks clowns are funny."

"Clowns are not funny. They're scary." She waved her wet fingers in the air. "I think you like him, too."

"I do not."

"You're blushing."

I covered my traitorous cheeks. "I don't *not* like him. How's that?"

"Ooooooh," she teased. "This is serious."

I stuck out my tongue at her, then found myself thinking about Devon for the billionth time that afternoon. "He *was* kind of cool today."

She nodded knowingly. "Because he likes you."

"He doesn't even know me."

"He'll have a chance to if you go to Benedict's." She wiggled her brows.

I couldn't help laughing. "You have such a one-track mind."

"Would it be such an awful thing if he did like you?" she asked. "I realize he's much too good looking. How any girl could date a guy with better eyelashes than hers is beyond me. But he is helping you get into Benedict's." She wiggled her eyebrows again. "This could be love."

"I've only known him a week."

"So? I've only known Jared a week and I think I'm going to fall for him."

"Who?"

"Jared is a camper on the performing-arts side. We met at the water fountain."

I rolled my eyes. "Why does that not surprise me?"

"He had a Handi Wipe, and he cleaned off the fountain head before he took a drink. It was so cute."

"That's not cute," I told her. "That's weird. Why do you like him?"

"Why not?"

I squeezed the fluffy pillow. "Do you have a pillow that's not so soft?"

"Why?"

"Because I want to throw it at your head."

She laughed. "You can't. You'll mess up my Preeba nails." She held up her left hand. Light from the pink chandelier glinted off the drying polish.

"What's Preeba?"

"Preeba is the name of my character. We chose pieces today for our final performance. I could have done *Our Town* with Anna, but instead, I chose a scene from a new play. I'm a genetically altered girl who lives on the far side of the moon. The dark side." She trailed her black nails dramatically down one arm. "I escape to earth and pretend to be normal. Only of course, there is no normal." She grinned. "It's the perfect character—I'm not who anyone expects me to be, but I'm still totally cool."

"Oh," I said. "Well, the polish works."

She studied her nails. "I'm thinking Preeba dresses angry Goth with a touch of playful."

"Playful angry Goth?"

"It's what everyone wears on the moon." She shot me

another grin. "I've already started memorizing my lines. My scene partners—Sean and Alec—they're way into it, too. It's going to be amazing." She frowned at her nails. "Maybe some red polka dots?" She grabbed a bottle of Ruby Red.

Megan had just picked her character and already she was morphing into Preeba. I reached for my necklace and pulled it out from under my shirt. Would it be so hard to morph into a Christian? It was just on paper. It wasn't as if it meant anything. "You really think I should do this?"

"How can you not?" she said. "Remember, you're not just doing this for you—you're doing this for me. I can't go to Benedict's without you."

I picked up the questionnaire. "It's not an actual lie."

"Exactly."

"And once I'm in, I can bring my matzo sandwiches during Passover and they won't be able to do anything about it."

"By then," Megan agreed, "you'll be the star orator and you can grow a beard and chant Hebrew and they'll all say 'Amen.'"

I took a breath. "Toss me a pen."

She did, and I punched the top with my thumb. I tried to write carefully, but my hand wobbled a little so it wasn't the neatest thing. But it was clear.

I'd just labeled myself a Christian.

I tried not to think what Zeydeh would label me if he ever found out.

CHAPTER 14

"Zeydeh, it was delicious," Dad said. He patted his stomach as if the bulge was all from tonight. Though, in all honesty, he had eaten like a pig—we all had. Except Zeydeh.

On Friday nights, to welcome in the Jewish Sabbath, Zeydeh always outdid himself in the kitchen. He baked fresh challah bread and cooked a huge feast. Mom and I lit the Sabbath candles, the men said the prayer over the wine, Zeydeh blessed Benny and me, and then we all said the *motzei*—the blessing over the bread. There was always an extra bounce in Zeydeh's step and when he brought dinner to the table, he'd hum a Jewish tune: *bim bom bimbimbim bom* . . .

But tonight, no bounce. No humming. The rest of us shot worried glances at each other through dinner, while Zeydeh seemed half asleep. Was it low blood pressure again? He did look kind of pale.

He perked up a little when I told everyone about the surprise meeting with Mrs. Yeats.

"I knew you were better than that boy," Zeydeh said, his eyes snapping open. "Didn't I say she was better, Skip? Didn't I say it the whole way home?"

"So you'll have an interview next week with Mrs. Yeats?" Mom asked.

I nodded. "I already filled out the questionnaire—it's due on Monday." I'd slid the folder under the stack of newspapers on the counter. I wanted to get it signed quick so I could stick it in my backpack and forget about it. Plus, if I was lucky, Mom would be tired after a long week and she'd sign without looking. "Can you sign it after dinner?" I asked.

"Of course." She laid a hand over her heart. "I'm just so proud of you."

"We all are, honey." Dad blinked, his eyes suddenly watery.

"Da-ad!" Benny groaned. "Crying is so not cool."

"If a man can cry over a chopped onion," Zeydeh said, "he can cry over his daughter's good fortune."

I smiled at Zeydeh. His eyes smiled back. "It's no more than you deserve, Ellie. I told you, didn't I, you would do great things in this world?" Then his gaze dropped back to his uneaten bowl of soup and his shoulders dipped.

Mom reached out and patted his arm. "You going to services tonight?"

Zeydeh shook his head. "I'll go in the morning. I'm a little tired tonight." He looked around the table. "If you don't mind,

I'll excuse myself." He stood, pushing up with his skinny arms as if his legs were too weak to lift himself.

"You sure you're okay?" I asked.

"Fine, fine. Just a little indigestion. I'll use the john, and be back to help clean up."

"We'll clean up," Mom said. "You sit down and take it easy tonight." She watched him shuffle out of the kitchen, worry in her eyes.

Even Benny stopped chewing to watch him go.

"Dinner was delicious," Mom called after Zeydeh.

"It was average," he called back, not bothering to turn around. Mom frowned and dropped her napkin on the table.

Cleanup was quiet tonight. Benny usually banged plates and rattled silverware clearing the table, but not now. I think we were all listening for Zeydeh.

I opened the dishwasher and took the plate Mom handed me. Dad had carried his to the counter, and he stood there waiting for me to have a free hand.

Above my head, I could feel Mom and Dad looking at each other.

"Should I say something?" Mom asked.

"I don't know what you can say," he answered. "It's the soup."

"The soup was fine."

"Fine, yes. Great, no." Dad mouthed the word "no" and Mom and I both darted glances toward the hall. No sign of Zeydeh.

"But surely he can make a few adjustments," she whispered. "He's always adjusting."

Dad leaned in, his voice a microwhisper. "I caught him this afternoon, standing over the soup pot with a pinch of herbs in his fingers."

"So?" Mom asked.

"So he just stood there. I washed my hands at the sink, poured a glass of iced tea, drank it, ate two cookies, and he was still standing there with the herbs in his fingers. Frozen. He didn't know whether to add them or not. I've never seen him like that."

Mom clenched her hands over her heart. "Did you say something?"

"I asked if everything was okay."

"And?"

"He said, 'Just stewing over my dreams.'"

Benny pushed through the middle of us and set another dish in the sink. "I'm going to shoot some hoops," he said, and headed for the back door.

Mom nodded, her eyes still on Dad. "That's what he said? That's . . . awful. You should have done something."

"Done what?"

Just then, we heard the shuffle of Zeydeh's shoes coming down the hall. Mom got out a rag and Dad pulled out some containers for the leftovers. I went back to loading dishes.

"Has anyone seen my glasses?" Zeydeh asked.

"On the counter, I think," Mom said.

I heard him rummage around the bowl of car keys. He cursed low, under his breath. Then the newspapers rustled and crunched. I was loading the last plate when it hit me.

Newspapers. Rustling. The application! I jerked up just as Zeydeh said, "What's this?"

My heart frog-leaped into my throat. "That's mine, Zeydeh."

"What is it?" He held out the slim white folder that Mrs. Yeats had given me that afternoon.

I flung the dishwasher door up so fast, plates rattled. "Just a folder."

"What kind of folder?" He flipped it open.

"Zeydeh!"

Mom and Dad stared at me, confused. I tried telling them with my eyes, but there was no way. No time. I had to get the folder out of Zeydeh's hands. If he saw what I'd written . . .

I lunged across the kitchen island and grabbed for it. But Zeydeh turned at the last second and I ended up with nothing but air.

He held the paper at arm's length and squinted at the words. "This is the questionnaire for Benedict's? What's so secret about—"

Then his voice broke and he leaned a hand on the counter.

"What is it?" Mom asked. "What's going on?"

Zeydeh turned, his eyes bulging. "You want to know? Ask Ellie. Ask your *Christian* daughter."

Then suddenly, he moaned and clutched his chest. His head dropped back and his eyes rolled shut. With a slight *whoosh* of breath, he collapsed into Dad's arms.

CHAPTER 15

"Zeydeh!" I screamed.

A sob caught in my throat, choking me as I rushed forward. Mom was already there, already reaching for his hand.

"Zeydeh!"

His eyelids fluttered, then opened. I nearly dropped to the tile, sweaty and light-headed with relief. *Thank you, God.*

"You didn't!" Mom said.

I blinked, wondering why Mom sounded almost . . . angry? Dad helped Zeydeh to his feet. I looked more closely, and realized his eyes weren't confused and unfocused like someone coming out of a faint. They were sharp and knowing.

"You were pretending?" Mom had her hands pressed to her cheeks. "I'm going to kill you, Dad. If you ever do that again, I'm going to hit you with one of your gourmet pans and kill you."

I gaped, fear heating into anger. "You were *faking*?"

"What?" he said, reaching for the questionnaire and waving it in my face. "It's okay for you to pretend you're Christian, but not okay for me to pretend to faint?"

"It's not the same thing," I snapped.

"Why isn't it?" he snapped back. "We're both pretending to be something we're not."

"What is going on?" Mom cried.

Dad scratched at his head, looking bewildered. "Okay," he said. "Enough drama. Family discussion. In the living room."

Dad led the way, then Mom, then Zeydeh. He had a little bounce in his step now. I wanted to kick him.

"That's not arguing fair," I muttered.

"You call yourself a Christian and you're surprised if it kills me?"

"You faked it."

"The pain is real, believe me." He smacked the sheet of paper on the coffee table.

"Would both of you just sit?" Mom ordered.

But Zeydeh wouldn't sit. He took up a spot by the far armchair. He held on to the back of the chair with one hand, a tiny tremor running down his arm. So I stood behind the other armchair. It felt like a staged debate: Zeydeh vs. Ellie. Mom and Dad sat between us, stationed on each end of the couch like judges.

"So what is going on?" Dad asked.

"Why don't you start with the questionnaire, Ellie," Mom added. She pulled the paper closer and tapped her fingers on the edge.

"It's from Mrs. Yeats," I said. "I told you about it at dinner. It's for the scholarship, and I'm supposed to fill it out and hand it in."

"You forgot to mention question number seven," Zeydeh retorted.

I glared at him. "Because I knew you'd blow it all out of proportion." I looked from Mom to Dad. "Number seven asks about religious affiliation."

Mom flipped over the paper. Her eyes widened. "You wrote 'Christian'?"

Dad frowned. "Correct me if I'm wrong, but aren't you the girl who had a Bat Mitzvah last year and proclaimed herself a Jew in front of everyone she knew?"

"I only wrote it because of something Devon said—about his grandmother."

"His grandmother?" Zeydeh planted a hand on one bony hip. "The woman is anti-Semitic, isn't she? A Jew hater?"

"She is not," I half shouted. "Why does she have to be anti-Semitic? Why is that always your first thought?"

He shouted back, wagging his finger, "*Besser fri'er bevorent aider shpeter bevaint.* Better caution at first than tears afterward."

Dad held up his hands. "All right, both of you. Let's try to get through this without raising our voices." He looked at me. "Ellie?"

"Devon just said she's really into her religion."

"And from that you decided to lie?" Zeydeh's eyes narrowed into a laser squint.

"Technically, it's not a lie."

"So now you're a religious technician?"

I swallowed a scream of frustration. Arguing with Zeydeh was impossible, but somehow I had to make him understand. "Dad *is* Lutheran."

"So they think you're Lutheran?" Mom asked.

"No," I said. "They don't think anything. The only reason it came up was because Devon saw Bubbe's necklace. He asked me about it, and then asked about the name Taylor because it doesn't sound Jewish."

"Did he ask why you don't have a big nose?" Zeydeh said, sarcasm as thick as an accent. "Jews always have big noses."

"He's not like that, Zeydeh. He was just asking."

"It's because of that camp. I said it was no place for a Jewish girl. No place for you."

"It's a great place for me."

"Then why are you lying?"

"I'm not lying! I'm telling half the truth."

Zeydeh wagged a finger at me. "A half truth is a whole lie!"

I looked pleadingly at Mom and Dad. "It's just a stupid questionnaire. What's the big deal?"

Mom gave me her teacher expression: pursed lips and wrinkled forehead. "You're using religion for your own convenience. Does that seem right to you?"

"It's just for the scholarship."

"But you're misrepresenting yourself," Mom said.

"Please!" I sputtered. "You told me to lie when I set up a

page on Facebook. Remember? I lied about my age and my address."

"That was for your safety," Dad said.

"And this is for my future!"

"You shouldn't have to lie to get into a school," Mom said.

"I also shouldn't have to answer questions about religion," I shot back. "But it's on the form, and I don't have any choice because it's a private scholarship offered by a private donor. Do you want my religion to be the reason I don't get in?"

Mom glanced at Dad. They both looked uncomfortable. *Point for Ellie.*

I turned to Zeydeh, pressing my advantage. "I thought you wanted me to follow my dreams?"

"What do dreams matter if you lose yourself along the way?"

I rolled my eyes. "I'm not going to forget who I am. I'm not going to forget Bubbe's family who died in the Holocaust. Mrs. Yeats isn't a Nazi. She's just a little weird about the speech team. You should have heard her talk. She thinks of the team as her extended family. Megan thinks she wants everyone to be a miniature version of herself. It's not that crazy. I'm sure plenty of Jewish families give scholarships just to Jewish applicants."

"Then you should apply for one of those."

"There aren't any for Benedict's," I said, punching the chair with my fist. "And last time I asked, no one in this family could afford the tuition. In fact, as I recall, you said if I wanted to go to Benedict's, I'd have to find a way to pay for it. So"—I crossed my arms in front of my chest—"I've found a way." I looked from Mom to Dad, daring either of them to deny it. But they couldn't. "It's just on this one form," I added, going for the big finish. "I filled out all the other paperwork for Benedict's and it never came up. Once I turn this in, that'll be the end of it."

"What if it comes up during the interview next week?" Mom asked.

"I'll tell Mrs. Yeats the truth. I'll even show her pictures from my Bat Mitzvah and chant the opening to my haftarah." I gave Mom a long, pleading look. "I know it's nothing bad. And just to be sure, I'll ask Devon about it first thing on Monday. It's not like I want to take money from someone who's anti-Semitic, either."

"I'm glad to hear that," Zeydeh muttered.

I clasped my hands together, begging for a yes. "Please, Mom."

Mom paused a long moment, then reached for the pen in Dad's front pocket. I held my breath until she'd finished signing.

"And if his grandmother *is* prejudiced?" Zeydeh asked.

"I'll call her a *szhlob* and spit in her eye."

"That's my Ellie," he said. But there was a flatness in his voice. And in his eyes. I'd make it okay with him again, I promised myself. No way could Doris Yeats secretly hate Jews. She wasn't like that. If only Zeydeh could have seen how nice she'd been. On Monday, I'd ask Devon, and Devon would explain, and Zeydeh would be cool.

And I'd be in at Benedict's.

CHAPTER 16

Monday morning was another scorcher. Beneath my white tank and navy capris, my stomach was full of butterflies when Mr. Swan dropped us outside Benedict's. The sun glinted off the glass doors, and the bronze handles had already heated from the morning sun. I pulled open the door, and Megan and I paused a second, breathing in cool air and letting our eyes adjust to the overhead lights. Groups of kids hung out around the lobby, some standing and talking, others sitting against the walls and listening to iPods or texting before assembly started.

As if there were a Devon sensor in my head, I glanced toward the far wall. He stood next to Peter Burrows, laughing about something. He wore a T-shirt as black as his hair over gray board shorts and black tennis shoes. I wasn't sure if black was a color, or every color, or the absence of color, but it was definitely *his* color. Before I could look away, his head turned and our eyes met. He smiled.

Holy crap.

Just when I decided he really wasn't all that great looking, he had to look like *that*. Megan and I walked toward the auditorium, but my heart thumped like we were sprinting.

"Did you catch that smile?" Megan said, under her breath.

"Unfortunately."

"He's hot for you."

I shook my head. "He's just hot."

Megan led the way down a row toward the back, and we took the middle seats—good for people watching. I saw Devon come in with Peter. They sat next to the aisle in the row in front of us.

"He's looking around," Megan said, nudging my shoulder.

"Who?" I asked, even though I knew she meant Devon. I knew he was looking around because I hadn't been able to take my eyes off him.

"I'll bet he's looking for you."

Before I could deny it, Mrs. Clancy cleared her throat into the mic. I cringed. She did it every morning—it was like starting the day with the croak of a dying frog.

"Good morning," she began. "Welcome to week two of camp. I will quickly run through announcements, as I have a special treat for you this morning." She said it with her usual puckered-lip scowl, so it was hard to feel too excited.

She launched into her update, and Megan leaned toward me. "Is that woman ever happy?"

"If she cracks a smile, her whole face might crumble," I whispered back.

Megan giggled, then clapped a hand over her mouth.

As soon as she'd read through the announcements, Mrs. Clancy cleared her throat again. Megan and I cringed in unison.

"Now for our treat," she said. "We will close today's assembly with a song of praise led by the Christian Society's very own Stephen Kayle."

I watched a man climb the steps, a guitar in his left hand. He had thinning blond hair and a round face. He waved at us and grinned. "Good morning, campers. I'm Stephen. Please stand and join me in song. You all know this one—it's our Lord's Prayer."

I stood slowly, and gave Megan a pointed look. *No, we don't all know this one.*

She shrugged. *What can you do?*

Guitar chords thrummed low and tinny from the podium. Stephen adjusted the mic, then began pounding out an upbeat tempo. It was pretty catchy, I had to admit. The music poured out from overhead speakers, and kids in front of us started clapping and swaying to the beat. I looked around. More swaying.

"That's right," Stephen called out, "let the Spirit move you."

I squeezed Megan's arm and asked, "Does he mean the *Holy* Spirit? Because there was nothing in the syllabus about dancing with the Holy Spirit."

Megan laughed. "Just fake it."

Stephen started singing, and I recognized the prayer as soon as he said, "Our Father who art in heaven." I didn't know

◇◇◇◇◇

all the words, but I'd heard them before on TV shows, and probably from Grandma Taylor.

After a slow start, the sound of voices built. Stephen beamed and strummed louder. I picked at my fingernails and waited for the magic word—*Amen*—because that would mean *The End*. Only, Stephen looked like he was just warming up.

That's when I realized the swaying had changed. Suddenly, everyone was swaying together like some kind of line dance. And instead of *Amen*ing, Stephen had launched into the beginning again. *Oh no*. The girl on my left swayed my way and shot me an irritated look when our hips bumped. I wasn't in sway mode.

I didn't want to be in sway mode.

I looked at Megan. She gave me a helpless shrug, and swayed.

Then, I don't know why, but I looked at him—Devon—and sucked in a sharp breath. He was swaying and clapping—and looking at me. He smiled. *At me*. I smiled back. Then he looked away and I looked away. I could feel the heat of a blush on my cheeks, and hear my heart thud louder than the music. It took me another second to realize I was clapping.

And swaying.

The girl on my left smiled at me. Like now we were swaying buddies. *Christian buddies*. What was I supposed I do? Tell her I was only fake swaying? How stupid would that sound? So I wobbled a smile back at her.

And then Stephen thrummed the guitar strings with a huge sweep of his hand and sang, *"Ahhhhmennnn."*

Thank God. I looked up then, a little guilty. *Sorry, God. You know it was a fake sway, right? No Spirit involved, I promise.*

"You are excused," Mrs. Clancy announced.

The auditorium filled with a wave of voices and the scuffle of eighty kids reaching for their packs. But there was an energy still thrumming through the air like the guitar music. Like the music had connected everyone.

Well, almost everyone.

It was like being in a crowd of kids when someone tells a joke, but you don't get the punch line. You laugh with everyone else because you don't want to look out of it. But you still *feel* out of it. I was glad to follow Megan through the double doors and back into camp mode. When we hit the lobby, I took a deep breath. The air felt cooler out here. Like I could breathe easy again.

Groups of kids veered off down the different hallways, and for a minute we had to concentrate on dodging traffic. Once we hit our hallway, Megan grabbed my arm and pulled me close. "Did you catch Devon giving you the eye? Because I did." She dipped her head so she could look over the edge of her glasses and bat her eyelashes. "As an expert in sizzle, I can tell he's falling for you. Big time."

I shook my arm free. "He is not falling for me."

"He might be," she said. "Instead of grilling him with questions, I'd be searing him with my lips."

I groaned. "When did you come up with that one?"

"This weekend. I've been saving it."

We reached my classroom door. Hers was farther

down—I could see Anna sitting on the carpet with a book in her hands.

"I've thought about this over and over," I said. I ticked off the points with my fingers. "One: Mrs. Yeats is a nice lady. Two: she's intelligent and sophisticated. Three: nice, intelligent, sophisticated ladies do not hate an entire race."

Megan adjusted a plastic pink flower she'd pinned to her raspberry top. "If you say so."

"As soon as I get a chance, I'm going to ask Devon to explain."

"Really?" Her eyes shifted to look over my shoulder. "Then here's your chance. He's headed this way."

CHAPTER 17

Before I could blink, my heart had jumped into hyperdrive. How could I ask him anything with my breath coming so fast? Besides, Peter was standing there, too, shaking orange Tic Tacs into his mouth. Plus, other kids were wandering up and the hallway was filling. A second after Megan took off, Sarah showed and we compared weekends. By the time we were done, Mrs. Lee had opened the door. Everyone pressed forward, but I hung back. My mouth turned dry as toast when I realized Devon had waited, too.

He tilted his head in greeting. "Wonder what torture Lee's got planned for us this week?"

"Can hardly wait," I said.

We shuffled forward a few more steps until he was so close I could smell the fabric softener on his shirt and feel the warmth of his arm next to mine. Breathe, I reminded myself. *Breathe.*

"My grandmother mentioned you this weekend."

I shot him a surprised look, but this close, all I could see was the underside of his chin. "What did she say?"

"She thought you were very poised." He paused. "Or did she say possessed?" He dipped his head just enough for me to see his half grin.

I rolled my eyes, and he laughed. Then we were in the door, and I went to my chair and he went to his. If we both went to Benedict's next year, would it be like this?

Totally and completely perfect?

I didn't have more time to daydream. Today we were picking topics. "This is the most important part of your oratory," Mrs. Lee told us. "Once you pick a topic, you'll spend all your time researching, writing, practicing, and performing. You'll live and breathe this topic for the remainder of camp, so you'd better make sure it's one that resonates with you."

She walked down each aisle and laid an index card on every desk. "Too often, oratory topics can become a lecture on a general world problem. Students scan the headlines and write a well-researched argument."

I found myself nodding. That was how we'd done it in middle school.

"What can sometimes be missing is the personal connection," Mrs. Lee said. "No matter how far reaching your topic, it should be one that also hits close to home." She walked back to the front of the room. "Remember, oratory is the only event that allows you to choose your subject and then argue any position you want. That's why it's called 'original.' So think about the issues facing you at school, at home, and in your clubs—and choose something that strikes an emotional chord. Use the index card I've provided to write down something that's affected your world. What was the last thing that made you angry? What scared you or excited you?" She nodded encouragingly. "If you're wondering how this will translate into a broader speech topic, trust me. It will."

For a few minutes, it got completely quiet. So quiet, you couldn't think, because all you could concentrate on was how quiet it was. Fortunately, I'd flashed on an idea in 0.1 second. A brilliant idea. I scribbled it down and read it over. I got tingles. Tingles were a good sign.

"Who wants to go first?" Mrs. Lee asked a few minutes later. "Nancy?"

Nancy nodded, her head bobbing up and down. She was like a hummingbird—always fluttering in high gear.

"My brother plays football at his high school," she began. "Last year, his coach wanted him to take a special PE class. But the only way to make it work with his schedule was to give up honors English for regular English. And he did it." Her hand flew up in disgust. "And my parents let him!"

"Okay," Mrs. Lee said as she wove her way through our desks. "What are the issues here?"

"How coaches pretend that education is important, but it's all about winning," Andrew said.

Tammy raised her hand. "How sports are treated as more important than everything else at school."

"Yeah," Ethan added, popping his retainer in. "If you're a good athlete, it doesn't matter what grades you get."

"Good," Mrs. Lee said, nodding. "There are important issues underlying what happened with Nancy's brother. And because it has meaning for Nancy, she has a better chance of creating that same emotional response in her audience." She looked around again. "Let's do a few more. Ellie?"

"This happened a few months ago," I began. "I needed a physical for school, so my mom took me to the pediatrician's office." I swiveled in my seat so I could look at everyone. "That's my doctor—still. I'm practically an adult, and I got examined in a room with Mickey Mouse wallpaper. It was humiliating. So it makes me wonder: there are special doctors for infants and old people; why aren't there special doctors for teens?"

"Interesting," Mrs. Lee commented. "Class, what are the issues?"

"Equal rights for minors," Sarah said.

Andrew added, "They call us young adults and treat us like babies."

"How our medical needs change through life," Peter offered.

Tammy's hand shot up. "And how the medical world is falling behind."

"Very nice," Mrs. Lee said. "I think you can take this in any number of directions, Ellie, depending on what captures your interest. It also has great potential for humor, which is definitely one of your strengths." She smiled, then looked around again. "One more?"

Hands went up around the room. Everyone's hand, in fact, but Devon's. Mrs. Lee must have noticed, too, because she walked over and perched on the edge of his desk.

"Devon?" She looked pointedly at his index card. He shrugged, and she slid the card out from under his fingers. She flipped the card over—it was completely blank.

"I don't know," he admitted. "Nothing hit me."

"Well, let's see if the class can help," she said. She folded her arms across her chest. "Tell us something you really like, Devon. Off the top of your head."

"Fast food?"

Everyone smiled, but Mrs. Lee seemed to take it seriously.

"Okay. What can you tell us about fast food?"

"I don't get to eat it enough."

There were a few laughs.

But not from Mrs. Lee. "Why not?"

He spiked a hand through his hair. "Because my mom thinks it's bad for me."

"Do you disagree with her?" she asked. "Do you feel her health concerns are unwarranted?"

He leaned back, stretching his shoulders in an exaggerated shrug. "My granddad grew up eating chicken-fried steak and mashed potatoes. How healthy was that? I think it's a double standard."

"Okay." She stood and faced the rest of us. "What do you think, class? Are there larger themes here?"

I raised my hand. "Has there always been some kind of junk food? Was it any better than what we eat today?"

107

Mrs. Lee nodded. "That would make a good informative oratory. What else?"

"Is comfort food healthier than fast food?" Peter said.

"Were the good old days really so good?" I said, then added, "And if food is so unhealthy now, why do people live longer?"

Mrs. Lee turned back to Devon. "What do you think? Something there to interest you?"

"Yeah."

She smiled and tapped his desk with her knuckles. "Good." She checked the clock. "It's almost time for lunch. I'll give you the rest of the afternoon to continue brainstorming topics. You're welcome to work at your desks, or if you'd prefer to brainstorm with a group, you can find a table in the lab. In fact, work wherever you like, as long as you're not disturbing other classes. You can use the next few minutes to arrange groups or organize your notes. By the end of today, I want everyone to have a topic and a list of potential issues to research. Tomorrow, I'll want to see your thesis statement."

Around me, everyone started moving. Sarah shifted back to talk to Tammy, and I heard Andrew behind me talking to Kim. I shut my notebook and just sat a minute, feeling a mix of relief and excitement. I had a kick-butt topic. *Nish-kosh-eh*, as Zeydeh would say—*Not so bad*. It had potential for humor, plus a serious side. I shut my eyes. *Benedict's, here I come.*

"You asleep?" a voice said. *His voice.*

I opened my eyes as a ripple of warmth worked its way up my neck. "Just thinking."

"You mean celebrating." Devon sat on the edge of Sarah's chair. "That's a great topic."

"It is, isn't it?" I couldn't help smiling.

"So you working with anyone this afternoon?"

I blinked. "Uh . . . not yet."

"You want to work together?" He shrugged. "You already have so many ideas on my topic, I won't have to come up with my own."

The ripple of warmth turned into a flood, and I let my hair fall over my face, hoping to hide the blush. "Well, normally I don't like to help the competition," I said lightly, "but since you're in such sorry shape . . ."

He laughed.

I got a whiff of orange a second before Peter appeared next to Devon. "Ready?"

Devon nodded. "We're going to grab some lunch. Where do you want to work?"

"I don't know," I said. "The lab?"

"How about the hall?" he said. "The window seat. Mrs. Lee said anywhere."

"Okay," I agreed. "Great."

After he left, I sat there a minute longer. Not because I was still thinking.

Because I wasn't sure my knees would hold me up.

CHAPTER 18

I got there first.

I wasn't going to—Megan said not to. Anna said definitely be late—make him wait. Then Megan added that if Devon got there first, he could watch me wiggle my hips on my way down the hall. That convinced me. I had no wiggle. I had no sexy hip move, no hair flip, and no eyelash flutter. And I didn't see why I needed to point that out to Devon Yeats.

So I was waiting for him when he came down the hall. He didn't have a wiggle either—which I had to admit was a good thing for a guy.

He dumped his backpack next to mine and sat across from me in the same spot as last week. "I don't know who invented fish sticks, but they should be shot."

"You got the fish sticks?"

"I was sick of pizza." He held his stomach. "Now I think I'm going to be sick of fish sticks."

I smiled. "Nice research for your oratory." I pulled out my notebook and a pen.

He leaned back, looking ready for a nap. "You're one of those organized team leaders, aren't you? The kind who writes out a schedule for everyone in the group with assignments and due dates?"

I pretended to be insulted, even though he was right. "And what about you? You're probably the type who says he's got it all under control, then shows up the day before a project is due carrying half-finished index cards smeared with chocolate."

"Not even close," he said. "French-fry grease."

I laughed. "As long as it's McDonald's fries."

"McDonald's?" He shook his head. "Burger King has the best fries."

"They have a funny aftertaste. Mickey D's are way better."

"You crazy?" he retorted. "They oversalt."

"The salt is the best part."

"Salt should be a personal decision."

The sun snuck in through a crack in the blinds, slanting lines of gold through his hair. As if he needed good lighting.

"What about ice cream?" I asked. "Dairy Queen or Baskin-Robbins?"

"Sonic," he said. "Awesome milk shakes."

"PC or Mac?"

"Mac."

I sighed. "Even I can't argue that."

"That's a first." He gave me a smart-ass grin and reached

for his notebook. I figured it was time to work, but then he shoved it behind his head like a pillow. "Have you always liked to argue?"

I nodded. "I was born with a big mouth. Literally. I have the baby pictures to prove it."

He laughed.

"Plus, I come from a family of arguers. You should hear my mom and my grandpa. They argue about everything." I tucked my hair behind one ear. "What about you?"

"I guess I inherited it from my dad. He competed in oratory, too."

He looked away when he said "my dad," and I could see his jaw tense.

My throat tightened. "I saw his name on some trophies in the lobby case. He must've been really good."

"Yeah," he said. "My mom donated them to the school after he died. She's sure I'll earn my own trophies to go next to his, and then go on to law school like he did."

"So you're following in his footsteps, huh?"

"Something like that."

"I think about being a lawyer sometimes," I admitted. "Arguing in front of a jury . . . making a case . . . someone wins and someone loses. I like that. But I also want to do something where you can change the way people think."

"About what?"

"That's the part I don't know yet."

"Something tells me you'll be good at whatever you do—you like to win."

"It beats losing." His eyes were so warm, I felt myself melting again. I wondered if Crayola could make a crayon that color? They could call it Hypnotic Blue.

"Maybe I shouldn't be working with the enemy," he said.

"Maybe," I agreed. "But then again, my grandpa always says, 'Keep your friends close, keep your enemies closer.'"

"Wise man," he said.

I had to laugh. "He also says, 'Everyone is beautiful if you squint enough.'"

Devon smiled. "He sounds cool for a grandfather."

I nodded, and reached for Bubbe's necklace. It wasn't there. I'd left it at home. I licked my lips, suddenly tense. Here was the opening I *hadn't* been looking for. But I had to say something. Put it to rest, once and for all. I let out a breath, fiddling with my forgotten notebook.

"Hey, so I've been meaning to ask. What did you mean the other day? That thing you said about your grandmother being weird about Jewish people? She's not a neo-Nazi or anything, right?"

"My grandmother in combat boots?" he said. "Can't picture it."

I relaxed a little. I couldn't picture it either. "I told my grandpa it was nothing bad."

"No. Nothing bad." He met my eyes for a second, then leaned down to retie a shoe. "The scholarship program is in memory of my dad, and my dad was a Christian. That's all it is."

"That's it?"

He leaned back. "Like I said, no big deal. It's just easier if she only knows about your Christian half."

It didn't exactly feel "easy" inside me, but what he said made sense. "I guess I can understand that," I said. I thought it through again, and felt myself nodding. *Yeah. Even Zeydeh would understand.* I smiled, and flipped to a clean page of paper. "I guess we should work, huh? We've got to turn in thesis statements tomorrow."

He pulled the notebook from behind his head. "If we have to." He fished a pen out of his pack. "So—special doctors for teens?"

"Yeah," I said, trying to focus. "I love the idea, but I have to show there's a problem with the system as it is. I need more than personal humiliation and Mickey Mouse wallpaper."

He raised a knee, balancing his notebook. "I thought that was pretty strong."

"Do guys have to go through that?"

"You mean personal humiliation?" He nodded in slo-mo. "Oh yeah."

"But you don't have to wear the little gown, do you?"

"You think we get boxers and a T-shirt?"

I grinned. "You, in a little gown with clouds on it?"

"It's worse for guys than girls. At least you're used to wearing a dress."

"Not with a gap in the back." I shook my head at the memory. "The doctor wore Tweety Bird earrings and called me sweetie. Then she wanted to discuss puberty."

"At my last physical," he said, "I had to put on the gown and hop on one foot."

A picture of it flashed in my mind, and I busted up laughing. Then he started laughing, too, and when we finally stopped, we were both breathless. I had to swipe at my eyes, where tears had leaked at the corners. "That's definitely got to be in my speech," I said, making a note. "If only the serious stuff were as easy."

"It will be," he said. "You can talk about depression among teens. STDs and condoms. And steroids are a big deal now. A lot of teens are abusing steroids and growth hormones. Are pediatricians trained for that?"

"Good point." I wrote fast, his ideas giving me new ideas of my own. In no time at all, I had a page of notes. "This is great," I said. And it was. I'd been so nervous about working with Devon, but it all just . . . clicked.

"So now it's your turn. Let's talk about fast food," I said.

"You think I screwed myself with the topic?"

"Are you kidding? It's a great topic. It all depends on what you want to accomplish. What's your thesis statement going to be?"

He thought a minute, his gaze shifting to the windows. The slivers of light had moved, and I wondered how long we'd been sitting here talking. He had a watch, but I didn't want to ask. I didn't want this to end.

"I want to strike a blow for fast food," he finally said. "It gets a bad rap."

"Mostly deserved," I had to admit.

"So you don't think I can do it?"

"Oh yeah, you can." I grinned. "It'll be fun."

He gave me a strange look.

"What?"

"You," he said. "Nothing scares you, does it?"

I swallowed. "Why? Is that bad?"

"No. That's cool." He paused. "You're cool."

I met his gaze—but just for a second. For a cool person, I suddenly felt way too warm. I looked back at my pad, taking a deep breath. "So, uh, junk food that isn't really junky. You can talk about food over the centuries and what people used to eat every day—cow brains and chicken feet and fried bugs."

He started writing. "Can you write my speech for me, too, while you're at it?"

I rolled my eyes. "Right. Mr. Unbeaten in Chicago last year."

He stopped writing and looked at me from the corner of his eyes. "You checking me out, Taylor?"

"No," I said. "Megan heard it from your grandmother. At the charity dinner where you met."

"Oh, right." He tapped a shoe against the seat cushion. "Kids Crisis Center. My grandmother forces me to go. There's another one this weekend she's been bugging me about—a fund-raiser for the Children's Theatre League."

"Megan's going," I said. "She asked me to tag along, but . . ." I shrugged.

"Maybe we should both go," he said. His voice was casual,

but my face still felt hot enough to set off a fire alarm. "We can sit together and argue about how bad the play is," he added.

I tried to sound as casual as he did. "Who says I'd sit with you?"

"We can fight about that, too."

I laughed.

"Come on. We better get back." He shoved his notebook in his pack and zipped it up.

I did the same.

Then he stood, slinging his backpack over his shoulder. "So we're on for Friday? Crappy food, old folks, bad theater?"

I fought a smile. "Well, when you put it like that."

"Good," he said. The look he gave me was so warm, sweat broke out on the back of my neck.

Then he reached out a hand to help me up. I slid my palm into his. Our fingers twined, and it happened again. A warm spark shot through me like a tiny bolt of lightning.

I sizzled.

But this time, I was pretty sure he sizzled, too.

CHAPTER 19

I knocked on Zeydeh's door, then opened it with my key. "Zeydeh?" I called. "It's me."

"In the kitchen," he called back.

"I've only got a few minutes," I said, weaving through his living room. "It's almost four o'clock, and I've got to get some work done before dinner."

Everything in Zeydeh's house was pure vintage—but not in a cool way. In an *old* way. Zeydeh said couches gave him a crick in the neck, so he'd never had one. Instead, there were four chairs—none of them the same—facing a round coffee table. The furniture was all in one piece, but just barely. Kind of like Zeydeh.

He was bent over the open oven, huge yellow mitts on his hands. "How was camp?" he asked.

"Great!" I dropped into a scarred wooden chair. "I picked

my topic. You've heard of pediatricians for kids and geriatricians for seniors? Say hello to teenatricians."

He half turned his head and raised an eyebrow. "Nice, very nice. I like it." Then he pulled out a pan.

I sniffed and wrinkled my nose. "Not the muffins again."

The oven door closed with a bang. He turned toward me and waved the tray under my nose. "Pomegranate and prune," he said. "First they pucker your lips, then they pucker your bottom."

I groaned and waved him away. "I am not going to eat one of those. None of us will. I don't know why you bother."

"They're Bubbe's favorites."

"I hate to state the obvious, but Bubbe's gone."

"So?" he retorted. "That means she lost her appreciation for a good muffin?"

I rolled my eyes. "There's nothing good about those muffins."

"They remind me of Bubbe. They cheer me up."

He loosened the muffins from his signature Calphalon pan. Zeydeh ate off plates as old as dinosaurs with chipped edges and scary food stains, but he had the best cookware money could buy. He tossed the muffins into a basket and brought them to the table.

"Why do you need cheering up?" I asked. "Is it still the soup?"

"What else but the soup?" His head dipped, as if it were too heavy for his neck. "I don't know why I bother. Mrs. Zuckerman will win again. Mrs. Zuckerman always wins."

"Come on." I slapped my hand on the table. "You're not giving up. You have two weeks, right?"

"Two weeks, two years . . ." He shrugged. "She's rubbing it in, Ellie. She knows."

"What do you mean, she knows?" Zeydeh had always been a little crazy, but he was starting to sound *crazy* crazy.

"She was here. This morning."

"Mrs. Zuckerman?"

"She came to the door with a letter addressed to me. Said the postman accidentally put my letter in her box. As if such a thing ever happens."

"It happens all the time." I reached for a muffin. It was hot on the tips of my fingers. Gray wisps of steam escaped as I broke off a piece and handed it to him. "Here, eat a little. You'll feel better."

He took the bit of muffin, but didn't eat it.

"So did you talk to her?" I asked.

"She wasn't here to talk. She was here to spy." Disapproval rumbled low in his throat. "She wanted to have coffee."

"Zeydeh, that's nice."

He lifted his eyes long enough to glare at me. "Who suggests coffee with the competition? Unless it's poisoned."

"Maybe she's trying to be friendly."

"Friendly, my *tuchus,* my rear end. She wants in so she can snoop around my kitchen." He sighed. "The only way my name will get on a plaque at the shul is when I'm dead."

"Don't say that!"

He waved a hand at me. "Enough with the bad news. Tell

120

me about camp. Did you talk to that boy?" He sat a little straighter. "What did he say?"

"Yes, I talked to that boy and his name is Devon." I ate a bit of muffin, then puckered when the tartness hit my tongue. I got up for some water. "It's because of Devon's dad. He died when Devon was a kid."

"What's his father got to do with a scholarship?"

I grabbed a cup off the draining board and stuck it under the faucet. "Nothing," I said, "except his dad was very involved in his church. The scholarship is in his memory, so religion is on the application." I turned off the faucet and took a drink.

Zeydeh scratched his whiskers. "I still don't like it. Religion should not be an issue."

"I told you it was nothing bad. Besides, Devon knows I'm Jewish. And he likes me just fine."

"What's not to like?" As if he couldn't help himself, his face softened into a mushy Zeydeh smile.

I reached over and hugged him, scratching my cheek on his stubbly chin. "I love you."

He pulled back and waved me off, but his cheeks looked pinker than they had in a while.

"I should go now," I said. "I promised Devon I'd help him come up with intro ideas. He's probably waiting for me to call right now." *Waiting. For me.*

"What's that smile for?" Zeydeh asked.

I smiled wider. "He asked me out for Friday."

"Devon?" His voice rose with his eyebrows. "You're too young to date."

"It's a charity event. I'm going with Megan's family, but Devon will be there and we'll sit together."

"You're too young to sit with a boy."

I laughed.

"Will his grandmother be there?"

"I think so. And probably his mother, too."

"Good. Then you can tell them both you're Jewish."

I planted a hand on my hip. "Stop trying to turn this into such a big deal."

"Hello, good to see you, I'm a Jew," he said. "What's the big deal?"

I rolled my eyes. "I'm going home now. You'll be over for dinner?"

"Who else will cook? Your mother?" His fingers tapped a nervous rhythm on the table, but when he spoke, his voice was soft. "You really like this boy, Ellie?"

I felt the answer flow through me—surprising, but as strong and as steady as my heartbeat: *Yes.*

"Yeah, Zeydeh," I said, my voice a little thick. "I really like this boy."

"I still say you're too young to date."

"Maybe it's time *you* go on a date," I said. "Next time she comes to spy, you should ask out Mrs. Zuckerman."

"Me?" He waved a hand in my direction. "I'm too old to date."

CHAPTER 20

"I'm about to kill myself," Devon said. He held a deep-fried beef chalupa with sour cream and cheese from Taco Bell. He raised it an inch from his mouth. The class stopped shifting in their chairs. The classroom, our makeshift tournament stage for this Friday, had never been so quiet. No one wanted to miss what he said next—even me—and the intro was my idea. Talk about helping the enemy. Even crazier—I wanted him to nail it.

Sizzle had short-circuited my brain.

And I wasn't even sorry about it.

Fortunately, I had two things going for me. One, Devon wasn't an applicant for the Benedict's Scholarship—he already had all the Yeats money he could want. Two, I did still want to kick his butt. Just for the fun of it. So I couldn't be completely mindless, right?

Devon opened his mouth, started to take a bite—then

stopped. "And when I do kill myself, I'm going to take some of you with me."

Today's presentation was just for the class. Mrs. Lee didn't want to spoil the final tournament for parents by letting them hear our intros now. But I hadn't missed Mrs. Yeats sneaking in the back this time.

"By eating this chalupa, I'm going to send heart disease, high blood pressure, and obesity through the roof," Devon said. "I'm going to impact the economic health of this country. I'm going to cause grisly deaths of the underage and undereducated in meatpacking plants. And that's just the beginning, according to authors such as Eric Schlosser of *Fast Food Nation*. The bookstore shelves are full of experts' books proclaiming our nation is spiraling toward processed death—all because of fast food. If only we could turn back time. Go back to the good old days. To the way our parents and grandparents used to eat. Those were the healthy days. Or were they? Were the good old days really that good? Is fast food really that bad? If this chalupa doesn't kill you, the truth just might."

Devon paused another second, made eye contact with everyone in the room, then took a bite of the chalupa.

The whole class burst into applause. *Nice.*

A second later, I felt a firm hand on my shoulder. Even as I turned, I caught the scent of roses. Mrs. Yeats smiled down at me. "One of his best intros. I believe you had something to do with that."

My heart kicked against my ribs. "I only helped him brainstorm."

She squeezed my shoulder gently, but I felt it to my bones. Felt warmth where her hand rested. "Humility is another quality we admire at Benedict's," she whispered.

Then she walked back to her chair.

Yes!

It was going so perfectly. Devon and I had spent every afternoon that week at our nook. We brainstormed ideas for our oratories, and talked about his old school and my old school and what it would be like at Benedict's. *Together.* The word "together" hadn't actually come up, but it was all I thought about. I'd imagined a million scenarios of our getting together. My favorite: Devon presenting me the trophy on stage and admitting he was completely smitten. Did guys say "smitten"? They should, I decided.

It wasn't all my imagination. Tonight was the charity theater event, and even if he hadn't used the word "date," Megan said it counted as one. By the time we started school at Benedict's, she predicted, we'd be going out.

When *we* started at Benedict's. I shouldn't say it like that, as if it was a sure thing. But it was getting closer. This afternoon, I'd meet with Mrs. Yeats. As long as I didn't blow it somehow, the scholarship felt like mine.

And I wasn't going to blow it. I was prepared—even for Question #7. If Mrs. Yeats asked about religion, I'd tell her how Grandma Taylor was on the board of her Lutheran church—that ought to score me some points. And if I didn't happen to bring up other things, like being Jewish, that wasn't lying. It was Selective Sharing. Mrs. Yeats didn't have to know everything. And Zeydeh didn't have to know that she didn't know. Fortunately, he was preoccupied with the ratio of celery to carrots in soup.

I couldn't believe the butterflies in my stomach. I wanted the interview to go really well. I wanted her to like me. Devon told me she'd had dinner at the White House once. Talk about a good person to have on your side.

When Mrs. Lee called my name, I stood, feeling invincible. My long, straight skirt forced me to take slow, even steps to the front of the room. I'd pinned up my bangs and rolled the rest of my hair into a bun. I looked older and more mature— or at least, that was the idea.

"I'm fourteen years old," I began. "I continue to face the horrible indignities of puberty. Changing body, womanly issues, acne, and bone growth. The teenage years are some of the most important and terrifying in the realm of growth and development. And how does the medical community respond to my needs? They send me to a pediatrician where I wait in a lobby with screaming infants and a video of *Snow White and the Seven Dwarfs*. I'm led to a room with Mickey Mouse wallpaper, magazines about puppies and kittens, and a gentle reminder on bright yellow construction paper not to chew the books. Then, a nurse tells me to strip down and put on a paper robe. With Mickey Mouse watching? I don't think so. It's humiliating. More importantly, it can be dangerous if pediatricians are not prepared for the unique biological and mental needs of teenagers. What, then, is the solution?" I asked.

"There are pediatricians for infants and children. There

are family doctors for adults. There are geriatricians for seniors. It's time the medical community reacts to the very real, very individual needs of teens. For the sake of our health—mental and physical—our society must train and prepare a new kind of doctor: a teenatrician."

I looked around the room, then smiled and bowed. The sound of applause swirled around me, my heart beating in time with the rhythm of it.

Yes! Yes! Yes!

When the bell rang for lunch, I waited for Devon at my desk. He'd been coming over to talk whenever we had a few minutes' break. Sarah had noticed—everyone had noticed. "You guys hooking up?" she had asked yesterday. I said we were just friends, and shrugged like it was no big deal. But the idea of it felt so big that I could hardly keep it inside. Devon and me—it hardly seemed possible, much less real.

I watched him angle around the desks on his way over. A shivery feeling ran through me, and I couldn't help smiling.

"Nice intro," he said, sliding into Sarah's seat as she got up. He gave me his smart-ass grin. "Good enough for second place."

I stuck out my tongue. "Very funny. And you have chalupa in your teeth."

He laughed, and draped an arm over the back of the chair. "You meeting with my grandmother?"

I nodded. "After lunch."

"I'll walk over with you, okay?"

"Okay."

Devon still ate lunch with Peter, and I ate with Megan and Anna. After all, we were just friends. But I couldn't stop myself from wanting it to be more than that. Which was why the scholarship had become even more important. Benedict's wasn't just about speech team. Now it was a chance to be with Devon, too.

Lunch flew by. I couldn't eat much and mostly listened to Megan and Anna talk about their scenes. When I dumped my trash and stacked my tray, Devon was at the door to the cafeteria, waiting.

I'd noticed that he'd started carrying his backpack on his left shoulder instead of his right. It was a little thing, but it meant that we could walk side by side closer—without any backpacks between us. Every time he did it, my stomach fluttered, and every hair on the back of my neck stood up and danced.

When had I started to like him so much? If you'd asked me two weeks ago, I'd have sworn he was the last guy I'd ever like. Now, he seemed like the only guy I'd ever like again.

"So we're on for tonight?" he asked.

We hooked a left through the lobby and down the hallway toward the offices. "Megan's picking me up at seven."

"Cool." He slanted me a half smile as we rounded the corner to Admin. The secretary wasn't at the front desk, and it didn't look like Mrs. Clancy was in her office, either. The door of the vice principal's office was half open. I couldn't see Mrs. Yeats, but I could hear her on the phone. "He sold the company? When?"

Devon and I exchanged a smile. One of those secret smiles you only shared with a guy you liked. Who liked you back.

"He sold to a Jew? My God, don't they already own a piece of everything?"

Mrs. Yeats's voice startled me back to earth. *What?* She had to be joking. She had to be talking to her best friend, who was Jewish, and they were joking.

I stared at Devon. "It's nothing," he mouthed, but he looked embarrassed. "Business stuff."

"Exactly," Mrs. Yeats said, with a short laugh. "And the country wonders why the financial markets are in ruins." She let out a loud breath. "If we have to, we have to. I need those printers delivered by August first." I could hear her tap a pencil on the desk. "It irks me, though. You know I hate working with those people."

It didn't sound like a joke. It didn't sound like nothing.

Those people?

"Uh . . . Grandmother?" Devon called.

A second later, I heard her say good-bye, and then she appeared at the door, smiling like nothing was wrong. Like she hadn't just said all those things. It felt like a snake had coiled around my windpipe. I couldn't breathe.

"I'm sorry," she said. "I didn't hear you come in."

"Ellie's here," Devon said.

"Wonderful." Then her perfectly tweezed brows lifted an inch. "Are you all right, Ellie? You look a little pale."

I didn't feel pale—I felt hot. My head pounded so hard, my brain felt sore.

"She's fine. Right, Ellie?"

I glanced at Devon. What was that look? Was that the eye version of a shrug? Was I supposed to shrug off what I'd heard? *What had I heard?*

Mrs. Yeats gestured to the office. "Why don't you come in? Have a seat."

Someone had to do something—say something. She had to know I was a Jew so she could explain. So she could say she didn't mean anything by it.

I looked at Devon. *Say something.*

His eyes urged me forward.

"Ellie?" Mrs. Yeats said again.

I swallowed hard, and followed her in.

CHAPTER 21

The theater lobby had been turned into something out of a fairy tale. There were thousands of tiny white lights glittering from every direction. They draped the walls and fell in strands from the ceiling, like falling snow. The people wandering around were just as glittery as the lights—lots of women in sequins and men with shiny, bald heads.

I'd borrowed a designer black dress from Megan, one that cost more than I made in a year of babysitting. It gathered at the shoulders with thick straps, and then fell in a straight line to my ankle on one side and my knee on the other. The material was so soft and sheer I felt like I was wearing pajamas. I'd clipped back the hair on either side of my face to show off a pair of diamond studs I'd borrowed from Mom. The finishing touch was a pair of black heels that hurt my feet but made my legs look hot, according to Megan.

Megan wore black silk pants and a long red cami with fake

fur around the neck and lace around the hem. She'd timed her visit to the orthodontist so she could get red bands to match her outfit.

Her parents had gone off to schmooze, and we'd found a semiquiet corner of the lobby to people-watch. I hadn't seen Devon and his family yet. I wasn't sure I wanted to. I still felt edgy and nervous after this afternoon, and I could tell Megan was worried about me. She kept shooting me looks and picking at the red skeleton charm on her bracelet.

"I'm not going to make a scene and embarrass you, if that's what you're worried about," I finally said.

"As if you could embarrass *me*." She twirled around the skeleton head. It had an evil grin outlined in rhinestones that twinkled every time it caught the light. "I'm just worried about you."

"I should have said something."

"Like what?" Megan asked. We'd been through this once, after camp, but we'd only had a few minutes until my dad showed. Then Megan had to go get her nails done with her mom, and there hadn't been any time to talk.

"I should have asked her what she meant."

"And admit you were eavesdropping? Nice way to start an interview."

"I couldn't concentrate the whole time. I don't even know what I said."

"But she was nice, right?"

I nodded. "She worried I was feeling sick, so she did most of the talking."

"See? That's nice."

"Yeah, but what she said on the phone wasn't nice."

"Which is why you and Devon need to have a serious heart-to-heart." She jabbed the air with a French-manicured nail tipped in scarlet red. "Just not tonight." She breathed in through her nose, like she was sniffing a batch of cookies. "Smell the air."

I sniffed. "It smells like air."

"It does not," she retorted. "It smells like a garden. You know the theme for tonight? 'Love is in the Air.' How's that for a romantic setting?"

"Megan—"

"Seriously," she interrupted. "You like this guy. I know you do. And he likes you. And here you are, in this amazing place, and music is playing, and you look totally hot. How can you let his grandmother wreck that? This is your chance."

"For what?"

"For romance. For love. For planting one right on his lips."

"I don't want to plant one," I said.

"Liar."

I sighed. I *was* lying. That was the worst part of it. "Why did she have to say those things?"

"People say stupid stuff all the time. I never told you this before, but my great-aunt Hilda used to say, 'If you want a good deal, you've got to Jew them down.'"

"That's gross, Megan."

"I know," she agreed. "I'd tell her so, but she's dead now."

She reached across me to a waiter with a tray of drinks. She grabbed two martini-style glasses and handed one to me.

Tiny bubbles rose to the top of the creamy drink. "What is it?"

"Peach juice with a splash of ginger ale."

I took a taste. The bubbles tickled my nose. It tasted like peach nectar from a can.

"Seriously," she continued. "Most of the time old people don't even realize they're saying something bad."

"Mrs. Yeats is not an idiot. She manages millions of dollars."

"That's not what I mean." She waved her drink at me, sloshing a little over the side. "It's like your saying you crossed your legs Indian-style."

"That's not meant to be an insult."

"Maybe it would be if you were Native American."

I rolled my eyes.

She rolled hers back. "Come on, Ellie. You've done it, too. Called someone an Indian giver. Or said you were gypped—how do you think Gypsies feel about that?"

"What about her saying 'those people'?"

"I know it sounds bad, but it could mean a million different things."

My fingers tightened around the smooth stem. "It was the way she said it. It was such a put down. And I just sat there through the whole interview. I never said anything."

"You're trying to impress Mrs. Yeats, not give her a lesson in political correctness."

"Devon told me it was no big deal. He said it was because

of his dad being religious. Now what am I supposed to think?"
My stomach started churning the way it had this afternoon.
Acid burned halfway up my throat. I felt sick. Sick and mad.
"Devon should have said something. It's *his* grandmother. Then
she could have apologized, and I wouldn't have to feel like this."

"Feel like what?"

I turned at the sound of his voice. He'd come up right
behind me. He wore a dark suit and a light blue shirt. His
eyes seemed to reflect back every light in the place.

"You look great," he said.

If only you didn't look so great. "Thanks." I kept my hands
tight around the glass. I wasn't sure what I'd do if they were
free—slug him or hug him.

"Hey, Megan."

"Hey." She flashed her red bands at him. "So, uh, I should
go check in with my mom and dad." She squeezed my arm.
"I'll come find you later."

I nodded and watched until her red shirt disappeared in
the crowd.

Devon slid a step closer. His teeth gleamed white against
his tanned skin as he smiled. "How you doing?"

"Fine." I tilted back the glass and finished my drink.

"How's the drink?"

"Fine."

He rocked back on his heels, and I could see him trying to
figure out what was going on. "You mad about something?"

"What do you think?" I countered, glaring straight into his
eyes.

He ran a hand through his hair, spiking up the edges. He tilted his head toward the door. "Let's go outside."

"Maybe I don't want to go outside."

"Okay." He crossed his arms, his eyes challenging. "Let's fight in here."

"No." I set my glass on a glittered tray. "Let's go outside."

"Great idea," he said sarcastically.

I pushed toward the lobby doors. The room had gotten really crowded in the last few minutes and it took about fifty "excuse me"s before I finally made it outside.

The moon hung low, a yellowish crescent in a blue black sky. The air was warm, but there was a tiny breeze that felt good on the bare skin of my arms. More people were standing around sipping drinks. I walked down some steps to a big round fountain circled by a wide cement bench.

I sat down. Then he sat down, leaving plenty of space between us.

The silence stretched out for a long minute.

"You going to tell me what's going on?" he finally asked. "Did something happen during the interview?"

"Yeah, something happened," I said, swiveling to face him. "And you were standing there with me. She said a totally crappy thing and you knew it. I could see it in your eyes." I searched his face. "Why didn't you say something?"

"Say what?" His eyes held mine as frustration rippled through his voice. "Was I supposed to tell her you're Jewish? You already told her you're Christian."

"I only said that because you told me it was no big deal."

"It doesn't have to be," he said.

"She was slamming Jewish people, Devon, and I'm Jewish."

"Half Jewish."

"What's that supposed to mean?" I said with a gasp. "I should only be half offended?"

His tanned throat worked above the pale collar of his shirt. "What do you want me to say?"

That was easy. I wanted him to say religion didn't matter. I even opened my mouth, but I couldn't make the words come out. After today, I knew religion did matter. What scared me was wondering how much.

I dipped my hand in the shallow pool of the fountain, skimming my fingers over the water. Tiny ripples spread in semicircles, chasing each other to the edge of the pool. "I know people say stuff like that without thinking, but it was the way she said it." I glanced up, wanting to catch his eyes, but he looked away.

I flicked my fingers at the water, widening the circle of ripples—making waves where there had been none. Was that what I was doing with Devon? I took a shaky breath. "I need to know, Devon. I need to understand what's going on with your grandmother."

He glanced back toward the theater. There was one other couple still on the patio with us, the man taking a last puff on his cigarette. Everyone else had gone inside. "I think the play is starting," he said.

I didn't move.

He sighed and turned back, his face in profile as he spoke

◇◇◇◇◇

to the night. "Look, I don't know what to tell you. We've never really talked about it. It's not the kind of thing that comes up at the dinner table. But she's made comments about Jewish people before . . . about business stuff mostly."

"So it's just business?" I asked hopefully.

He paused as if he wasn't sure what to say, or maybe he didn't want to say anything. But then he shrugged. "It's not just that. She gets an expression on her face. I can't describe it, but it's like she's pissed about something."

"What?"

"I don't know," he repeated. "I figured it was something bad that happened once with my grandfather's business."

"And now she hates Jews?"

"No. It's not like that." He shifted a little closer. "It's nothing against you personally."

A car's horn honked in the distance. Across the street, jazz played on the outdoor speakers of a pizza place.

"Maybe I should talk to her, explain things," I said. "I know she likes me. Maybe if I tell her I'm Jewish, she'll understand."

He shook his head. "It wouldn't do any good. She's not going to award the scholarship to a Jew. It's just the way she is."

"My grandpa would say good riddance, then."

"What would you say?"

I stared into the dark blue of the fountain, twirling a new pattern with my fingers. "I don't know." I could hear the confusion in my own voice. "I don't want to lose my chance for the scholarship, but then I think of him shaking his finger and telling me to spit in her eye." I sighed. "I guess it sounds lame, caring what my grandpa thinks. I get mad sometimes because he's so bossy and opinionated, but I don't want to disappoint him, either. It's hard to explain."

"You kidding? You don't have to explain it to me—I've got it times two."

I pushed back a piece of hair the breeze had worked loose. "What do you mean?"

"My mom and my grandmother both have this plan for me. Basically, I follow in my dad's footsteps, whether I want to or not." His lips twisted into a sad smile. "Even oratory— it's my event because it was my dad's event."

"But you're so good at it."

"I don't hate it, but it wouldn't be my first choice."

"What would be?"

He flicked his fingers through the fountain. A waterfall of drops spattered the cement, then evaporated in the heat. "Last year, my high school had a radio station. Nothing big. I think the signal reached all of five miles. Mostly, it was for school announcements. But a few of us put together a radio show for Saturday nights. We did whatever we wanted. One night, we'd rant on the lame blogs we found; the next night, we'd do a show on a kid who got jumped for being poor. It was cool." He caught my eyes and smiled. "Like oratory, without having to write a paper or quote sources."

"You know, radio is an event at a lot of speech tournaments."

"It's not an option for me. My grandmother doesn't think it's a serious event."

"But if you love to do it . . ." I let my words trail off. "What about your mom?"

"She likes my doing oratory." He stretched out his legs. "It was really hard when my dad died. It took a long time for my mom to be okay again. This thing with oratory . . . it's hard to explain. But it's like I'm becoming him all over again. She's really happy about it, and I don't want to mess that up."

"But it's not what you want."

"It's just how it is."

"What if you said something?" I asked.

"I've tried. It doesn't do any good. It's like swimming against the tide. Wears you down."

I rubbed the back of my neck, loosening the tight muscles. "We're supposed to be looking ahead, you know? We're the next generation, the future. But it's like our parents and grand-parents want us to live in the past. My grandpa and I argue about it all the time."

"Who wins?"

I smiled. "No one wins against my grandpa. Besides the fact that he's crazy, he brings up the Holocaust. How can you argue against that? My grandmother had relatives who died in concentration camps. It always comes back to the past."

"Maybe that's what happens when you get older."

"So what do you do," I asked, "when you want to live for the future?"

His eyes were smoky blue in the dark. "You do what you're doing. You go after what you want."

"Benedict's, you mean?"

He nodded.

I frowned, my thoughts turning back to his grandmother. "I just can't believe she wouldn't like me because of my religion. It's like something out of a history book, something that doesn't happen anymore. You know?"

"She's old, Ellie. Old people still think old thoughts. I don't think the same way. You know that, right?"

Just hearing him say it made me feel better. It also made me want to reach over and hug him. Instead, I curled my hands tighter around the smooth edge of the bench. But I couldn't help leaning in his direction. "It just doesn't make sense. I mean, if she knew I was Jewish, then what? Does she think that suddenly I wouldn't be talented and smart? Suddenly I wouldn't be worthy of Benedict's?"

"So prove her wrong."

"How?"

"By winning."

The thought spread through me like heat in my veins. What if Devon was right? If I won the tournament, I'd win her respect. I'd prove myself. Then, when I told her I was Jewish, she'd see how wrong she'd been.

"It doesn't bother you that I'm lying to your grandmother?" I asked.

He got quiet. "Normally it would."

"But?"

141

"But this isn't normal." He slid his hand over the top of my hand, then curved his fingers around mine. My mouth went dry. His eyes flickered at me, questioning at first, then more intense when I slid my fingers between his.

"I don't normally fall for girls who are so much trouble."

I fought a smile, then gave up. It felt like a sparkler had gone off inside of me, shooting light and heat in a million directions. "Me, trouble?"

"From day one, you wanted to kick my butt."

"You're the one who challenged me to a cuckoo duel."

He fit his palm to mine, and squeezed my hand. "You have to go to Benedict's, Ellie. It's a huge pain if your girlfriend doesn't go to the same school."

I shivered in the warm night. "Girlfriend?"

"If you say yes." He shifted so close our knees touched. So close I could feel his breath on my cheek. "Not that you've ever said yes to anything in the two weeks I've known you. And I know it's only been two weeks, but—"

"Yes," I breathed.

He paused, his slow smile making my heart stall. Then he leaned forward and kissed me.

It felt like magic, sitting there. Like something in a movie—the moon above, the quiet night, his hand in mine. Only better. Only *real*. I didn't want to move. I didn't want it to end.

But the doors were banging open and people were coming out, heels tapping on the concrete, conversations rising and falling. I pulled back. "We missed the first half," I said, embarrassed.

"Best play I've ever been to."

I laughed.

His fingers squeezed mine again. "We cool?"

I nodded.

He looked toward the open doors and the streams of people walking into the night. "You sure?" he asked, a catch in his voice.

"Why?"

"Because in another minute, my grandmother is going to be here."

I pulled my hand free and ran it through my bangs. "Great."

"You can tell her you're Jewish after you get into Benedict's. We'll tell her together. Okay?"

I pushed back my worries. "Okay."

He looked toward the stairs again, then reached for my hand. Doris Yeats stood at the doorway. I could tell the moment she spotted us.

My muscles tensed, as if I were preparing for a punch to the gut. It seemed unreal. How could the sweet-looking woman smiling at me hate me?

"I need to warn you," he said. "She wants to invite you to Sunday brunch."

"Sunday brunch?" I repeated. She had started down the stairs toward us.

"She likes you, Ellie," he said urgently. "She knows I like you."

I took a deep breath, shifting my gaze to him.

"Just say yes, okay?"

I knew Zeydeh wouldn't say yes. Just the thought of him tugged at my gut. But I knew it was a tug toward the past. Walking toward me was the future. "I'll say yes," I said.

Only I didn't know I was saying yes to more than brunch.

CHAPTER 22

The flagstone felt rough on my bare feet as I stepped outside. The patio was shaded, but I still squinted against the morning sun. The intense glare made the landscape rock sparkle and had burned the Bermuda grass to a yellow green.

Dad looked up from his potting bench, and his mouth dropped open. "What are you doing awake so early?" He looked up at the clock hanging on the patio wall. We'd only had it a few weeks, but already the copper had oxidized and turned a speckled green.

I yawned and shuffled around a bag of potting soil. I dropped into a lounge chair. "I forgot to close the blinds last night. The sun got me."

"What time did you get home?"

"About eleven. Mom said you were already asleep."

He went back to pouring soil into a wide, round pot. "Did you have fun?"

"Yeah." It wasn't the most descriptive word, but then again, I wasn't going to tell my dad about Devon. I wasn't going to use the word "magic." Or confess that I was completely in love and that Megan had been so right about Respecting the Sizzle. I couldn't tell him it was the most perfect night of my life, right up until the second when Mrs. Yeats had shown up, opened her mouth, and ruined everything.

Dad's work area was a mess. Tools and gloves and empty pots were stacked on the shelves of the hutch, and bags of soil and fertilizer sat half open and leaking over the flagstone. But somehow, out of the disaster area, he created amazing things.

"That looks pretty," I said. He'd combined white zinnias with orange marigolds. I watched him tamp down the earth around the flowers. It always relaxed me, watching him work with flowers. It felt simple, natural. Why couldn't life be like gardening?

I let out a long breath.

"What's wrong?" he asked.

"Why does something have to be wrong?"

"You just thought it would be nice to sit outside in hundred-degree weather on a Saturday morning and watch your dad plant flowers?"

I played with the hem of the shorts I'd thrown on with the cami I slept in. "Mrs. Yeats asked me to brunch tomorrow."

Dad paused, looking up. "Really? Does she invite all the Benedict's applicants?"

"I've kind of started hanging out with Devon."

"Ah," he said. "I take it you like Devon?"

I nodded, my heart answering with a squeeze. "He's really cool, Dad."

Lines fanned out from the corner of his eyes as he studied me. "And he thinks you're really cool?"

"He asked me to be his girlfriend last night."

"What?" He shook his head. "You're too young to have a boyfriend."

"You sound like Zeydeh."

"Probably because Zeydeh also knows the rules: no dating until you're sixteen."

"I know," I said, shifting deeper in the chair. "We're just going to hang out. Talk on the phone, that kind of thing."

"I suppose that's all right." He puffed up his chest, and showed off his biceps. "But if I have to, I'll give him my scary-dad routine."

I laughed. "You have no scary-dad routine."

"I can work on one," he said, depuffing. "So what's the problem?"

"Turns out it's not just Sunday brunch." I looked at him through the curve of my eyelashes. "As long as I'm joining them for lunch, Mrs. Yeats asked why didn't I also join them for church."

His hands stilled. "Uh-oh."

"Yeah." I swallowed. "It's a Lutheran church, so she's sure I'll feel right at home."

"You did give her that impression." He gave me a sharp look, then went back to his flowers.

"I'm thinking I can chalk it up to religious exploration.

147

◇◇◇◇◇

You and Mom always say Benny and I should be open-minded."

He set the finished pot at my feet and reached for another one. "Is that what this is really about? Open-minded, honest exploration?"

"It could be," I said slowly.

"Or it could be a lie, which is why you feel bad about it."

"Who says I feel bad about it?"

"You're not still in bed sleeping like a baby."

I sat up, folding my legs under. "You've done it, too," I said defensively. "Remember a few months ago when those Bible-thumpers came to our door?"

"No." He sprinkled some plant food into the pot.

"You told them you were Jewish, which you're not. Just to get rid of them." I twisted my hands around the metal armrests. "People lie about their religion all the time. Even Zeydeh's grandfather changed his name when he came to America."

"It's not the same, Ellie."

"Why isn't it?" I asked. "I watched that show on PBS—Jews lied about being Jews to get into colleges all the time."

"Because there was discrimination—quotas—it was their only chance."

"Well, this is my only chance," I said stubbornly. "Isn't discrimination still discrimination?"

He paused again. "Is that what this is?" he asked. "Discrimination?"

I rested back in the chair again, only every one of my muscles suddenly felt stiff and tight. "It turns out, the weird thing she has about Jewish people . . . is that she doesn't like them."

"You serious?" He stared at me, his mouth hanging open. "What happened to your spitting in her eye?"

"Devon said it wouldn't do any good," I admitted. "The only way to fight discrimination is not to let it affect me."

"But it will affect you, Ellie. It already has."

"But why should it? Religion is supposed to be about good things. Besides, Christians and Jews have a lot of things the same, like the same God. The Christians just have one more dead guy than we do."

He wiped the back of his hand over his chin. "That's one way of looking at it."

"Shouldn't religion be about being a good person? What's it matter what you call yourself? It's all the same thing."

He rested his hands on the edge of the pot, the tips of his fingers as brown as the dirt. "It's not the same, Ellie. Grandma Taylor isn't a Christian because that's what she calls herself. She's a Christian because she believes that Jesus lived and died for her sins. She finds great comfort in her beliefs, and in the church."

"Then why don't you go to church?"

He wiped his chin again, this time leaving a thin line of dirt. "Do you know who George Bernard Shaw was?"

I frowned. "A writer?"

He nodded. "He once said, 'The best place to find God is in a garden. You can dig for him there.'" He looked at his plants. "This is my church. This is where God lives for me."

"It makes Grandma mad, doesn't it?" I said. "That you're not more religious? Was she mad when you married Mom?"

He shook his head. "Not really. The hardest part for her was when you and Benny were born. She wanted to baptize you."

"You mean, put water on our heads?"

"Something like that. She worried you wouldn't go to heaven."

"Of course I'm going to heaven." I made a face. "But maybe she should worry about Benny. I have my doubts."

He smiled.

I leaned down and wiped a clump of dirt from the edge of the pot he'd finished. "I wonder if God cares? Or if it seems dumb from up there? You know, how things feel so big on earth—like a house seems big, but when you get up in a plane, it's barely the size of a bread crumb."

"I don't know," he said. "But I do know that no matter how much distance you try to put between yourself and a lie, it's still a lie."

I swallowed. "I promised Devon I would go."

"It's your choice, Ellie. Just be sure you're thinking it through."

I could feel his eyes on me, even though I didn't look up. "I wish we were more like flowers." I traced a finger over an orange petal shot through with a curl of yellow. "Zinnias and marigolds are different, but look how nice they are in the same pot."

He sighed. "Amen to that."

CHAPTER 23

The Lamb of God felt like the church Grandma Taylor attended when she came for visits. High ceilings made the church feel bigger than it was, and a little awe inspiring even for me—and I wasn't in the mood to feel awed.

The wood pews were polished to a shine, and I was pretty sure that lemony scent was Pledge. A row of stained-glass windows caught the morning sun, and prisms of light floated on the far wall like a moving watercolor.

Devon's family had the third row. His grandmother sat on the middle aisle, then a friend sat next to her, then Devon's mom, then Devon, and then me. Even with the carpeted aisles, I could hear people filing in around us, but no strangers sat in our row. Not that there were any strangers at Lamb of God. That's what the minister had said when Mrs. Yeats introduced me.

It wasn't totally different from a synagogue—except for

the sculpture of Jesus that hung over the altar, the collection of crosses arranged on one wall, and the Christian Bible in every pew. In other words, okay yeah, it was different.

I'd told myself there wasn't anything to feel bad about. It was just a church service and it didn't mean anything. That's what I would have told Zeydeh—if I'd told him I was going. Instead, I got Benny to do Juice Duty and figured Zeydeh would think I was sleeping in. I smoothed down the skirt of my green dress. I just wanted to avoid an argument, but it still felt like he was in my head making old-man noises and squinting in disapproval.

Devon handed me a Bible. I realized everyone else already had one out and in their laps. I smiled to show I was okay, and he winked to show he was okay with me not being okay.

I flipped open the book and tried to focus. In synagogue, the prayer books opened to the right, and Hebrew would have filled half the pages. But I only knew a little Hebrew, anyway. Maybe if Devon and I kept dating, I'd want to go to church with him. But would I always be trying to look Lutheran, whatever that meant?

Can you help me out here, God?

I closed my eyes. The choir had started a song, but the music faded in my head as I pictured God. When I was little, I always thought of him sitting in heaven on a chair, like Abraham Lincoln in his Washington monument. Even though I knew it wasn't really like that, I still pictured him that way, right down to the beard.

You know what's going on, God. It's not like I'm trying to change teams or anything. This doesn't make me a traitor to Zeydeh and Bubbe and every Jew who's been killed in the past five thousand years. I just want to prove to Mrs. Yeats that I deserve the scholarship. You wouldn't have given me the talent if you didn't want me to use it, right? Just so we're clear, God, that it's okay, because if it isn't—well, just give me a sign if it isn't.

I opened my eyes and looked toward the pulpit. There was no flashing sign saying, "Ellie, you're a traitor." The sculpture of Jesus hadn't suddenly woken up and pointed his finger at me. For a second, I studied the sculpture with the blank stone eyes. What would Jesus have been like? The eyes were shadowed and sad, the head tilted down.

I'd never really known what to think about Jesus. One of the first things I'd ever been told about him was that I'd killed him.

I was seven years old, in Miss Kennedy's second-grade class.

It was a Friday. I could still picture it like yesterday. It was too hot and sunny for the playground equipment, but the teachers had set up games to play under the shade structure. I was standing in line for hopscotch and picking at a scab on my elbow.

Lisa Fernando turned around and twirled one of her braids at me. "You killed Jesus," she said.

I opened and closed my mouth five or six times, then said, "What?"

"And you're going to H. E. double toothpick. Hell," she added in a whisper, and stuck out her tongue.

I stuck out mine, too, and told her she had ugly knees. But

153
◇◇◇◇◇

after school, I took one step into my house and burst out crying. Zeydeh was in the kitchen. He dropped the ball of dough he'd been kneading and pulled me into a floury hug. Then he took my hand and led me to the couch. He sat down, pulled me onto his lap, and waited for me to cry it out.

Zeydeh said some emotions were too big for words—they spoke only in tears. That day, my tears had a lot to say.

"So," he asked when I was done, "tell me what happened."

"Lisa Fernando said I'm going to hell."

"She said *what?*" he sputtered.

More tears poured from my eyes. "She said I killed Jesus and I'm going to burn for it."

"Rubbish," he grunted.

"It's true," I sniffled. "They told her in church."

"And did they also tell Lisa Fernando that Jesus was a Jew?"

I nearly fell off Zeydeh's lap. "He was? Really?"

Zeydeh nodded. "As Jewish as you and I. Would he send a fellow Jew to you-know-where?"

I smiled at the face he made and wiped at my runny nose. "Grandma Taylor says Jesus is coming back."

"Well," Zeydeh said, "then we'll invite him to join us for Shabbat dinner. I'll make my famous noodle kugel. You think Jesus's mother made a kugel as good as mine?"

I thought about Jesus eating noodle pudding with cinnamon and raisins, just like we did. "So I can go to heaven, too, Zeydeh?"

"Of course, my little one," he said, rubbing a hand over my wet cheek. "But not, I pray, for a very long time."

◇◇◇◇◇

His face went dark then, the way it did when his mind had gone somewhere sad. I knew he was thinking about Bubbe being in heaven.

"Zeydeh?" I asked. "You can cry, too, if you want."

He blinked. His eyes cleared and he hugged me. "Today, I will only cry tears of happiness that I should have a granddaughter like you."

I hugged him back.

And the next day, I delivered my first oratory—to Lisa Fernando on Jesus and noodle kugel.

◇

I sighed, blinking myself back to the present. I studied the sculpture again. *Did you eat noodle kugel, Jesus?* It was strange to think of him as more than a symbol—to think of him as a person. If Jesus were here right now, would he come to Lamb of God to pray? Or would he go to a synagogue? Did *he* feel bad, being here in a church?

Did I?

I thought about it as if I could feel Christianity on my skin, breathe it into my lungs. It didn't feel bad being here, just different. Just not . . . me. I studied Jesus again, and suddenly, it hit me. Our connection. He and I were the only two Jews in the place.

By the time the service ended, I felt better. There'd been no sign from God. Zeydeh might not understand, but obviously God did.

I drove with the Yeatses to the Shadow Mountain Resort

for brunch. From the front seat, Devon's mom filled me in on who would be joining us, while in the backseat, Devon held my hand.

We were shown to a private room with windows draped in green velvet and a long table with eight settings of white china, polished silverware, and cloth napkins. The manager had come forward when he'd seen Mrs. Yeats. He'd followed us in, his hand on her elbow—nothing was too much trouble for her. It took me two minutes to decide I could get used to this—three waiters hustling around asking if I wanted anything. What more could I want? If I was looking for a sign, wasn't this it? Just the fact that this was so perfect had to mean something.

I followed Devon to the long white tables of buffet food. Steam rose from covered silver dishes, and with every step we took, the smells got better and better. I filled my plate with eggs Benedict and bright yellow mango and three kinds of pastries all dripping with icing. And bacon. A pile of crispy bacon. Why not? We never had it at home, mostly because Zeydeh kept kosher and bacon was *treyf*—unclean. But it wasn't as if I kept kosher, too.

When we got back to the table, everyone was already seated with their plates full and coffee steaming out of dainty white cups. There were full glasses of orange juice for Devon and me. We'd been given the two seats at the far end of the table. It felt like brunch for two, and we ate our way through our plates of food, talking about camp and the other kids and their oratory topics. Then we got onto the topic of fast food, and it wasn't long before we were laughing more than we were eating.

"That's what we need," he said, "a fast-food breakfast buffet. Just think of the possibilities."

I licked bacon grease off my thumb. "I am, and it sounds gross to me."

"You kidding?" he said. "Pancake sticks with fake butter and french-fried eggs."

"What about taco-flavored muffins?" I asked. "Or biscuit-gravy burgers?"

That made him laugh. "And for dessert—sausage chunks and cheese cereal."

I was wiping tears of laughter from the corner of my eye when Mrs. Yeats set down her napkin and asked, "What's so funny down there?"

I tried to catch my breath.

"Just ideas for my oratory," Devon said.

"Which I've yet to see," Mrs. Yeats replied.

"You'll see it during the final tourney in two weeks."

She shook her head with mock impatience. "Do you share ideas with your family, Ellie? Devon is very secretive with his."

"I try not to share," I said. "But my grandpa usually manages to get it out of me."

"Ah yes," Mrs. Yeats said. "Devon mentioned that you're very close to your grandfather. He lives with your family?"

"Just down the street."

"Your father's father?"

I wiped the napkin over my mouth. "My mother's father." My stomach suddenly felt full in a bad way.

"Then he's not a Taylor?" she continued.

I shook my head. I tried taking a sip of water, but even my throat felt full. Zeydeh had once tried to teach me how to play chess. I didn't have the patience for it, but the one thing I liked was how you figured out your opponent's next move before they even made it. It felt like that now . . . like I could see where she was headed, but I couldn't see how to stop her.

"What is his name, Ellie?"

Checkmate. His name ran through my mind: Shmuel ben Yakov in Hebrew, Samuel Morris Levine in English. About as Jewish as a name could be.

"It's very possible we might have met," she added. "I'm very involved in the senior community. Perhaps his name will ring a bell."

And it would. Just not the one she expects.

I paused, not sure what to say. Was this a sign from God? Was I meant to tell the truth? The whole truth? What if I did? Would she tell me to leave? My stomach curled into a painful knot. Maybe a half truth? *Half the truth—for half a Lutheran?* And suddenly the words were coming out. "His name is Sam," I said. "Samuel Morris."

She looked thoughtful. "I don't believe I know the name, after all."

I tried to look disappointed, and a second later the subject was dropped.

And there was no bolt of lightning from God.

◇◇◇◇◇

Fifteen minutes later, Mom showed up to drive me home. Devon's mom had offered to give me a ride, but Mom wanted to come. She wore a summer dress with splashes of pink flowers and her only cool pair of sandals, which sucked, because I couldn't borrow shoes that Devon had seen on my mom's feet.

She shook hands with everyone, and she and Jennifer Yeats got into a discussion about teaching. Devon's mom had worked in a school library years ago and was thinking it might be time to go back. "It's changed so much," Mom said. "Everything is computerized and Internet based." They talked until the waiter came to clear. Then we said our good-byes and Doris Yeats walked us to the front of the hotel. Devon came, too.

A huge chandelier hung in the center of the lobby, with teardrop crystals hanging below each light. They reflected prisms along the wide glass windows that overlooked the entrance. I could see Mom's VW parked along the circular drive.

"I'm so glad Ellie was able to join us," Doris said to Mom. "It's wonderful that we share the same beliefs."

Mom nodded, but slowly. Really slowly. "It was kind of you to invite her," she finally answered. Then she had to turn away, because Devon's mom was saying how nice it was to meet her. And the two of them started talking again, and then Doris reached for my hand and clasped it between the two of hers.

"I hope you enjoyed our service," she said.

◇◇◇◇◇

"I did," I answered, and realized it wasn't even a lie. "In fact," I said, smiling to myself, "I've never felt closer to Jesus."

As soon as the words were out, I realized Mrs. Yeats wasn't the only one listening. My mom had finished with Devon's mom. From the pinched look around her mouth, I could tell she'd heard every syllable.

CHAPTER 24

Mom slammed the car door shut and shot me an angry look. "Never felt closer to Jesus?" she repeated. "What was that about?"

I strapped on my seat belt, breathing in the pine freshener. "I did feel close to Jesus," I said defensively. "As a fellow Jew." I kicked my shoes off and rolled my toes into the gray square of carpet at my feet.

"You completely misled that woman and you know it."

"Can we just go home?"

She started the car and slowly inched around the drive. I could still feel the heat of her stare. "What is going on here, Ellie? I thought you were going to tell her at the interview. She seemed completely unaware of your Jewish background."

I laid my head back along the vinyl. The air conditioning was blasting and I could feel the strip of cool air where it hit my neck. "Can we please be quiet? My stomach doesn't feel good."

Mom shot me another look as she merged onto the freeway. "It's probably your conscience."

"Or the three pastries I ate." *Or the bacon. God, are you mad about the bacon?*

I heard her breath hiss out. "What happened to coming clean?"

"I decided not to."

"So now you're lying to everyone?"

Sudden anger flashed through me. I sat up, tugging at the seat belt strap across my chest. "Why is it me that's wrong? Why am I the one who's supposed to have a conscience? What about Doris Yeats? She's the one who's discriminating against Jews, and no one seems to think that's wrong."

"Of course we do!"

My eyes filled with angry tears. "Then be on my side for a change!"

Mom's hands squeezed the steering wheel. "I am on your side. But two wrongs don't make a right."

"You don't understand."

"Of course I do," she snapped. "More than you know." She shoved a piece of hair behind her ear, and didn't seem to notice when it popped right out again. "You aren't the only one who's struggled with religion. When I was just a few years younger than you, I pretended my name was Le-Vine so I could be Christian like everyone else."

I tilted my head, watching her hands clench and unclench on the wheel.

She sighed. "We'd just moved to Arizona. I didn't want to be different. I already felt so lonely and awkward. I wasn't like you, Ellie. I wasn't confident and outgoing. So I lied. I pretended to have Christmas and Easter like all my friends."

"So what happened?" I asked.

She slowed down for our exit. "There was one other Jewish kid in my school. She ratted me out—said Le-Vine was really Levine and she'd seen me at temple." She shook her head. "That was Margot Wasserman and we're still friends after all these years."

"So it worked out okay?"

"It'll work out for you, too." She gave me a quick smile as she shifted lanes. "I hoped in this day and age, it would never come up. I think a part of me liked that when I married your dad, I knew you would be Jewish, but also have a foot in the Christian world." She reached across with a hand and ran her fingers along my cheek. "It's terrible to think that someone might hate your child just because of the religion you gave them."

Tears filled my eyes again. "I just want the scholarship, Mom. I want to go to Benedict's and be on the speech team, and I want Devon to be my boyfriend, and I want to be a part of all that. Why can't I be a part of all that?"

"Oh, honey," she said, her voice an ache. She pulled onto our street, then into the driveway. She ran a hand through my hair, sweeping the bangs from my face. Her own eyes were full of tears, too.

"I just want to be a kid at camp like all the other kids," I said. "I want to get up there and do my oratory and be judged like everyone else. And I want Mrs. Yeats to keep looking at me the way she does, like I'm a prize she's going to win for Benedict's."

"You are a prize," she whispered.

"I'll tell her after I win the scholarship. I promise. By then, maybe it won't matter when she finds out I'm Jewish."

"Ellie, you can't continue to mislead her." Her eyes were wet and shiny, but her lips were set in a thin line. "I'm sorry, but this has gone far enough. As your parent, I have to speak up."

"What?" I swiped a hand across my cheek. "What do you mean?"

"I'm calling Mrs. Yeats. She needs to know the truth."

"You can't!" I cried. "She'll give the scholarship to some-one else."

"Not if she's the kind of woman you say she is."

"But she'll know I've been lying. She'll hate me."

I wasn't sure why, but that thought made me cry even harder.

CHAPTER 25

Was the phone ringing right now?

Was Mrs. Yeats picking it up? My ears strained to hear what I could only imagine. My mother was calling this morning. While I sat in the plush auditorium with the voice of Mrs. Clancy droning on like elevator music, my mother was getting ready to destroy my life.

Was the phone ringing right now?

"You okay?" Devon whispered. He sat on my right, and next to him was Peter and then Nancy and the whole Benedict's group. Would they be sitting with me tomorrow?

From the stage, Mrs. Clancy paused. "And now for our morning prayer. In Jesus's name we pray."

I bowed my head and folded my hands together. I wasn't wearing Bubbe's necklace anymore, so I knew I blended in. I didn't even have to pretend to look like I was praying. I was.

I figured if everyone else was praying to Jesus, then maybe God had more time for me.

I squeezed my eyes shut. *Can't you stop her, God? I know she's my mother, and it's in the Ten Commandments that I'm supposed to obey. But you're her Father in heaven, so that means she's supposed to obey* you, *right? So can't you tell her to stay out of it? Visit her in a dream and tell her we've talked and you've got it covered. I am going to tell Mrs. Yeats, God. You know I am—as soon as I win.*

Was the phone ringing right now?

Benedict's was a world I'd always dreamed of—dignified, privileged, special. I'd only ever had a window into this world. But now, a door had opened and I could see my way in. And waiting on the other side was everything I wanted.

Including Devon.

How could I stand to go back?

How could my mom do this to me?

Was the phone ringing right now?

The final oratory tourney was next Thursday, only ten measly days away. I would've been so good, nothing else would have mattered. Mom just didn't understand. I mean, every kid kept some things secret. Megan had gone to a counselor for two years—she didn't exactly announce that to the world. A guy at my school had a brother in prison—you could bet he wasn't putting that on any applications. We all kept things hidden. It wasn't a bad thing. It was survival. But thanks to my mom, Mrs. Yeats would think I'd been lying, and someone else would get my future.

"Amen," Mrs. Clancy said.

"Amen," I murmured along with everyone else. I lifted my head, as kids stretched and grabbed their packs. Devon reached over for my hand. From a row up, I saw Sarah catch the movement. Her eyes widened . . . *wow*.

Yeah . . . wow. I gave her a weak smile. As if I needed another reminder of all I had to lose.

"You stressing?" Devon asked.

"I'm too stressed to be stressing. I'm numb," I said. I stood and followed everyone down the aisle. "I'm dead. Or I might as well be."

Devon pulled me along, leading me toward our class. "Maybe your mom will give you a break."

"She said I've had enough breaks." She'd refused to budge; her only concession was that Zeydeh didn't need to know. Let him think I'd been the one to tell Mrs. Yeats, as I should have.

"Maybe Grandmother won't be here today. The computers are on order. It's not like there's anything for her to do until they're delivered."

I looked up, suddenly hopeful. "You think?" But a second later, a flash of silver hair caught my eye from the far end of the hall. I squeezed Devon's fingers. "It's your grandmother."

Mrs. Yeats made her way toward us, coming closer and closer even though I dragged my feet slower and slower.

Had my mother called yet?

"Hey, Grandmother," Devon said.

"Acknowledging me in the halls?" She gave him an amused smile. "Such an honor." Then she looked at me. "Ellie, I believe

I have something for you." She thumbed through the stack of folders in her arm, and pulled one free.

I nodded, swallowing hard. Probably my application, with a big, fat, red "DENIED" stamped across it.

"It's a schedule of fall classes," she said. "I thought you might want to take a look."

My eyes widened so much they hurt. I flipped open the folder. "Benedict's Course Selections." I flipped it shut. It was too awful . . . holding in my hands what I couldn't have. Because as soon as my mom called—

"By the way," Mrs. Yeats added, "your mother called this morning."

I stopped breathing. "She did?"

"The call was forwarded to my cell phone. I'm afraid the voice mail was garbled. For some reason, we're in a bit of a dead spot for cell phones, and I don't always get clear messages. Did she want a call back?"

"No!" I blurted. I hugged the folder to my chest. "I mean, no need to call her back. She, uh, just wanted to thank you again for yesterday."

"My pleasure," she said. Then she nodded and walked on.

I grabbed Devon's arm, mostly so I didn't collapse. "Did you hear that?"

He nodded, but instead of the grin I expected, he was frowning.

"What?" I asked.

"That was weird." He stared at the retreating back of his grandmother.

"What was weird?"

"She doesn't have phone problems."

"Then why would she say she did?"

"I don't know." He shifted his backpack. "That's what's weird."

I rolled my eyes. "So what?" I kissed the folder, too happy to care if I looked insane. "She gave me a class schedule, Devon. That means I'm still in the running."

He nodded, but the frown didn't ease up. I pretended not to notice. As Zeydeh would say, "Don't spit in the face of good luck." All I could say was, "Hallelujah."

I must have said it a million times during the day.

I said it to Megan when I told her we might be carpooling next year.

And to Mom, after I told her Mrs. Yeats had given me a schedule of classes.

And to Dad, when he said Mrs. Yeats must not be weird about Jews, after all.

I even said it to Zeydeh.

Lucky for me, "hallelujah" is completely nondenominational.

$\diamond$

The rest of the week flew by—every day better than the one before.

We started research, and I created fifteen bibliography cards when Mrs. Lee only required ten. Devon took the computer next to mine each afternoon. I couldn't stop myself from blushing, and I had to pretend it was from the heat of the computer screen. Just having him next to me was distracting enough, but then he would whisper little fast-food tidbits that made me laugh.

"Did you know cow's milk is mostly pus?" he asked. "Did you know sweetbreads are the thymus gland of young animals? Did you know young animals have thymus glands?"

We spent the whole day together and then half the night on the phone. Megan complained she had to book an appointment to talk to me. But she was busy, too. The final speech tournament was next week, but the performing arts group was presenting their scenes this Friday night. She'd morphed into Preeba with a vengeance and started wearing miniskirts and fishnets to camp. (The romance with Jared from the water fountain had fizzled out. Turned out Jared had used Handi Wipes at the water fountain to help with chronic canker sores. Not even Megan thought canker sores were sexy.) Anna had started blurting random lines from *Our Town* in the middle of a conversation. She got to do her scene perched on a ladder and couldn't wait.

Me, either. I wasn't going to miss Friday's performance for anything. Mom and Dad were coming, too. Zeydeh hated to miss it, but he wanted to go to synagogue. Maybe he'd find the soup answers he was seeking in the weekly Sabbath prayers.

Zeydeh was still in a funk. I hung out with him every morning before camp, and I had to force him to drink his juice. He'd started looking pale and tired and . . . old. He'd spread out every cookbook he owned, printed recipes off the

Internet, and gone to the library to research the history of matzo balls. I felt bad for him, I really did, but after twenty minutes discussing the anatomy of a taste bud, I was thrilled to skip out of there and go to camp.

I'd stopped looking for signs from God—at least the bad kind. There'd been no lightning bolts, no locusts, no frogs, no nasty plagues. I figured I was home free.

Until Friday afternoon, when disaster struck.

In person.

◇

"Dogs eat their own vomit as part of a healthy diet," Devon said.

I glanced up at him from where I crouched on the carpet. "Please tell me you're not putting that in your oratory."

Just as we were packing up for the day, I'd dropped my whole stack of index cards. They'd sprayed out on the carpet, a few sailing under the desks. I gathered up two more.

He pointed behind me. "You missed one over there."

"Thanks," I muttered.

The rest of the class had left a few minutes ago, but Devon had stayed to help. Not that he'd been any help. I reached for the last card, then stood.

"It's a nice tie-in to nature," he said.

"It's disgusting!" I shoved the cards in my folder, and then into my pack.

He laughed again. "I'm still going to compare the fat content of a cow's brain to a burrito."

"That's it for me and burritos."

He swung his backpack to his other shoulder and followed me out to the hall. It was amazing how fast the school emptied, especially on a Friday afternoon. Only one person stood in the lobby. It wasn't Megan. She must already be out in the truck waiting for me.

"You're not going to be mad, are you?" Devon asked.

I shot him a confused look. "Mad?"

"When I beat you?"

I punched his shoulder and he laughed. "No thymus gland is going to beat a teenatrician."

"Ellie!" A voice boomed down the corridor.

I tripped over my own feet, grabbing Devon for balance. *No, it can't be!*

But it was. The white shirt and dark pants, the wispy gray hair, the grizzled cheeks, and a grin that meant trouble.

"Your grandpa?" Devon whispered.

My heart thudded. "Is your grandmother here?"

"I think so," he whispered. "But it's okay. She's in Admin."

"I've got to get him out of here. Before he ruins everything." I hurried to the lobby. He stood waiting, every crooked tooth showing in a grin. "Zeydeh, what are you doing here?"

"I came with your father. I had wonderful news that couldn't wait, Ellie. A matzo ball breakthrough." He looked at Devon. "Who is this?"

"This is Devon Yeats. Devon, this is my grandpa." I reached for Zeydeh's arm, ready to lead him toward the door. But he shook me off and held out a hand to Devon.

"Devon, a pleasure to meet you."

They shook hands, until Zeydeh's thick brows dipped into a frown. "I look old and decrepit? I look like I'll break?"

Devon flashed me a questioning look, and then turned back to Zeydeh. "Uh, no?"

"Then why such a limp handshake? I won't crumble."

They shook hands again and then Zeydeh laughed and slapped Devon on the shoulder. Zeydeh winked at me.

I was going to kill him when we got home. "Where's Megan?"

"She's in the truck with your father. He's got marigolds and didn't want to leave them in the heat with the air conditioning turned off. I was sent to find you."

Volunteered, more like it. "Well, we'd better go then, Zeydeh. You can tell me your good news in the car."

"Your father can wait a minute while Devon and I have a chat."

"A chat?" My voice rose with the panic I was trying to keep in. "No. No chatting, Zeydeh."

He waved me off and grinned. "So you're ready for the tournament?" he asked Devon.

Devon nodded. "Getting there."

"I saw your eulogy, you know. It was good. Not as good as Ellie's, but good."

"Zeydeh!"

"What?" he said innocently. "I can't say you were better? I'm not saying he was *farkakte*."

I grabbed Zeydeh's arm. "All right. We're going now."

"What does *farkakte* mean?" Devon asked.

"Nothing," I said.

"Of course it means something," Zeydeh retorted, standing fast as if he'd put down roots. "It's a little Yiddish." He grinned. I hadn't seen him this happy in weeks. Zeydeh, this happy, was trouble.

"Do not say it," I warned.

Now Devon was grinning. "Say what?"

"*Farkakte* means sh—"

"ZEYDEH!"

"What?" He rocked on his feet, grinning ear to ear. "It's such a terrible word? I should say doo-doo? Poopies?" He winked at Devon. "Where's the dignity in that? I'm a grown man."

Devon burst out laughing.

"I like him," Zeydeh said to me, as if Devon wasn't there. "He's got a nice laugh."

"He's not laughing," I said. "He's clutching his stomach so he isn't sick."

Zeydeh ignored me. "It's a day for laughter, Ellie. A day to celebrate."

"Great. Let's go and we can celebrate." I glanced down the corridor. Still empty.

It was like he hadn't heard me. "You won't believe what happened," he said to Devon. "I took a nap this morning. I never nap, but today I napped. And who should I see in my dream, but my dearest departed wife, Miriam—Ellie's bubbe."

"You always see Bubbe."

"Not like this." He shook his head. "You remember your bubbe, before the cancer? Her silver hair, her cheeks like red apples, always so round, but soft and puffy like fresh dough?"

"I remember."

"Well, this Bubbe looked like a fashion model. Not a single roll of fat under her chin, and cheekbones like a young woman. Thin. I've never seen your bubbe so thin."

"That sounds nice." I glanced back down the empty hall.

"Nice?" he retorted. "Who dreams they starve you in heaven?" He shuddered. "I couldn't shake the vision. I woke up. I sat in the chair and wrapped myself in Bubbe's afghan, and then it came to me: fat! Not enough fat in the soup!" He clapped his hands with a loud smack. "That's been the problem. A little schmaltz—a little chicken fat—to give the soup some depth."

"That's wonderful, Zeydeh."

"It's a miracle is what it is. I already made a pot this afternoon. Even without time for the broth to settle overnight, it's ambrosia. My heart is singing, Ellie. Even my liver is doing a dance."

Then he pulled out of my grasp and started stepping side to side, in a Jewish dance step. I glanced at Devon, but he stood there, watching and grinning. Encouraged, Zeydeh snapped his fingers, lifted his elbows like two chicken wings, and sang nonsense words in his off-key voice.

"Devon?" A sharp call from the end of a hallway stopped us all, even Zeydeh. Doris Yeats was locking the door to the

Admin offices, but obviously wondering about the crazy man in the lobby. "Is everything okay?"

Is this what a heart attack felt like? I couldn't breathe, and red spots flashed behind my eyes. "We have to go, Zeydeh."

"Everything's fine," Devon called back.

Zeydeh squinted down the hall. "Is that your grandmother? I'd like to meet her."

Of course he would, I thought in a panic. He thought she knew all about him and our Jewish roots.

"Yeah, uh . . ." Devon swallowed. "She's really busy locking up."

"Nonsense. How busy can she be?"

"Zeydeh, please!" I yanked at his arm, pulling him a step toward the door.

"Careful," he snapped. "Or there'll be two of me."

Devon's eyes widened as if he'd just had an idea. "You can meet her tonight. At the performances."

I shook my head, still tugging on his arm. "Zeydeh's going to services tonight."

He squinted from me to Devon. "Perhaps I will come."

"But you always go to services!"

"I'll go in the morning." He pulled his arm free and straightened his shirt sleeve. "I'll tell your father you'll be out in a minute." He walked stiffly out the door.

I watched him go, then buried my hands in my hair. "What are we going to do now?" I hissed. "He'll meet your grandmother tonight."

Devon shook his head. "She's not coming tonight. She has

another event she couldn't get out of. She's videotaping the performances."

My shoulders sagged with relief. "Thank God. But we have to figure out something for next Thursday—for our tournament. He's going to insist on meeting her."

"We'll think of something," Devon said. "If we don't, the *farkakte* will hit the fan."

CHAPTER 26

We were going to be late.

"Mom!" I yelled. "Dad!" I flipped off the bathroom switch and headed for the kitchen. I'd tried curling my hair—complete disaster—and then had to wash it again. Having a boyfriend added at least twenty minutes to the minimum time needed to get ready. I'd worn a deep purple V-neck tank, a white skirt I borrowed from Megan, and platform sandals that showed off my newly painted purple toes. Another reason I was late.

"Mom?" I yelled again.

"Wardrobe malfunction," Mom yelled back from the direction of their bedroom. "Give me five minutes."

"We don't have five minutes." I strode toward their room, pushed open the door, then stopped. Dad had his face pressed in Mom's armpit. "Ew!"

Dad looked up and grinned. "I'm trying to fix your mother's

zipper. It jammed." The green dress had a long side zipper. An inch from the top it had stuck and I could see the material on one side jutting up. Dad tried sliding the zipper side to side.

"Careful," Mom said, "don't pinch my fat."

"What fat? You're thin as a rail."

She puckered her lips. "Oh, honey, that's so sweet."

I made a gagging noise.

They both laughed.

"Can't you wear something else?" I asked. "We're already late."

"I would if I could get this dress off, but it jammed too high. Besides, it'll take me as long to change as it will for your father to fix the zipper."

I sighed and leaned against the door to wait.

"Why don't you walk over to Zeydeh's," Mom suggested. "Make sure he's ready. We'll drive down as soon as I'm unhooked."

It was a short walk, even in two-inch heels, but I walked fast so the heat couldn't melt off my makeup. A few minutes later, I was knocking on Zeydeh's door. He hadn't said anything else about this afternoon, but he still wanted to come with us to watch Megan. Benny, on the other hand, had arranged to play hoops at a friend's house so he wouldn't have to tag along.

"Zeydeh?" I knocked again.

"Come in," he called. "It's not locked."

I pushed open the door. "Mom and Dad are running late. I came to see if you were—" I choked on my own breath. For a second, I just stared, my brain not believing what my eyes were seeing. "Zeydeh?"

"You were expecting Moses?"

He stood proudly in the center of his living room, arms held wide as if to say, "Look at me." And I was looking. In horror. "What are you doing?"

"Waiting for you." He flicked a speck of nothing off his coat sleeve. "I'm ready."

"Ready for what?" I sputtered. "An audition for Rabbi of the Century? It doesn't even look like you!"

He wore his usual white shirt and dark pants, but tonight he'd added a long black coat that must have been a thousand years old. Dangling from his waist were the knotted threads of his *tallis*—a prayer shawl I'd only ever seen him wear in synagogue. On his curly hair, a small round yarmulke was pinned into place.

"Of course it looks like me," he said. "I am a Jew. I look like a Jew."

"From two hundred years ago!" I said. "That's not how you dress."

He peered down at himself. "What? You don't like the coat?" He tugged proudly at the collar. "I bought this coat in Brooklyn fifty years ago. Two dollars and fifty cents—can you believe it? I've been saving it for a special occasion."

"What occasion is that?" I snapped. "Ruining your granddaughter's life? You can't go like that."

"How else should I go?" He gave me his innocent look. "Should I wear a cross and pretend to be a Christian?"

My stomach coiled into a fist. This was planned. Of course this was planned. My teeth clenched, holding back a scream of anger and fear and frustration. "Why does everything always have to be about you and religion and what you want? Can't this one thing just be about me?"

"This *is* about you," he said. "About who you are—a Jew, Ellie, a Jew! And yes, I want everyone there to know it."

His jaw jutted out, and I could tell I wasn't the only one who was angry. Well, too bad. This was *my* life, not his!

"Mrs. Yeats, you mean."

He shook a finger at me. "She shouldn't need my old coat to tell her what she should already know. But somehow, even though your mother assured me the truth had come out, it seems that Mrs. Yeats is still in the dark. How you managed that, I don't want to know."

"Please, Zeydeh!" The heat of helpless tears gathered behind my eyes.

"I'm at the school today and suddenly it's clear. You're embarrassed Mrs. Yeats should see me. Not just embarrassed, but worried. Crazed. And I ask myself—why? Suddenly, I know. My Ellie who speaks up about everything, suddenly says nothing." He stepped forward, his eyes fiery. "I want to know why!"

"You know why," I said. "For the scholarship."

"Of course, the *scholarship*." He rolled the word in his mouth like something bitter. "The scholarship offered by the nice Mrs. Yeats. She only asks religious questions in honor of her dead son. No big deal, you tell me. Except, why do you

181

◇◇◇◇◇

nearly break my arm shoving me out the door today?" He took in a long, broken breath. "I'll tell you why. Because she does not like Jews. And rather than stand up for who you are, you pretend to be someone you're not."

"That's not fair, Zeydeh." I grabbed the back of a chair and squeezed as hard as I could, an edge of panic building behind my anger. "You're not looking at this rationally."

"Now you're saying I'm irrational?"

I blew out a hot breath, trying not to let my thoughts get twisted up in Zeydeh's words. "Even if she is anti-Semitic, why should I suffer for that? Why should I let her prejudice affect me and keep me from what I want?"

"This is your argument? Two wrongs make a right?"

"I'm not doing anything wrong. Isn't there a Yiddish saying, 'You don't have to tell everything you know.'"

"You can twist words to make them sound pretty, but it doesn't cover the ugly truth." His eyebrows bunched up so his eyes were like shadowy pockets, deep and unsettling. "All your life we've talked about speaking up. About standing up for yourself. Now, when it matters most, you suddenly become silent. If you can't see this, you're not only lying to Doris Yeats, you're lying to yourself."

"I'm going to tell her, Zeydeh. Next week, when the scholarship is mine. It'll mean more then because I'll be in at Benedict's. Everyone will know it. I can speak up then, when it really counts."

"If you're silent today, you will be silent always."

"Great," I muttered. "Another Yiddish saying."

◇◇◇◇◇

"*My* saying," he retorted. "And here's another: 'If you're silent today, why should anyone bother to listen to you tomorrow? By tomorrow, it is too late.'"

I let out an angry growl. "You're not listening to me now!"

"If you have something to say, I'll listen."

"Then don't do this." I reached out a hand toward him. "Don't wreck this for me—not when I'm so close."

"Close to what? To denying yourself? To shaming your past?" He folded his arms over his chest, unmovable, unyielding, in every way.

Helpless anger boiled through my veins and flooded my head with red heat. Whatever was holding me together let go. I let go. "Fine," I shouted. "You want to wear that? Fine. Mrs. Yeats isn't even going to be there tonight, so be my guest. Make a fool of yourself. She's not even going to be there."

He drew himself up straighter. "Then I'll wear it again next week to your performance."

My heart thundered with rage. I was nearly dizzy with it. "No, you won't—because you won't be there. You hear me? You're not invited. Stay home, Zeydeh—stay out of my life!"

He stepped back. At first, I thought it was the force of my words, pushing him, unbalancing him. But then I saw a sheen of sweat suddenly bead on his forehead. He raised a hand to his chest. His fingers shook.

But I'd seen this trick before.

"Don't try it," I said. "I'm not going to fall for the same trick twice."

"Miriam," he said. His eyes blinked. "Miriam."

Miriam? Why was he asking for Bubbe? A trickle of unease lifted the hairs on the back of my neck. "Zeydeh?"

He blinked again. "Ellie," he said softly. Then his eyes clouded, and he fell back. It happened in the time it takes to snap a picture. It felt like that in my mind. Like the snap of a camera. The flash of a bulb. Then, a sharp picture seared into my brain.

Flash. One arm hitting the corner of a chair and twisting up.

Flash. His head hitting the hard wood floor.

Flash. His face tilted toward me, his eyes dead.

Zeydeh dead.

It all happened in the space of a breath. A single, horrible breath that screamed inside my head, and then fell silent. My ears strained for a sound. My heart, my soul, strained to hear the sound of a breath. The sound of life. There was nothing.

Nothing.

I had killed him. I'd killed my Zeydeh.

I started to scream. I screamed into the emptiness of the house, the emptiness of Zeydeh's slack face. I screamed— until the door suddenly burst open and my dad rushed in.

"Ellie!" he shouted. Then he saw Zeydeh.

And I collapsed, wishing I were dead, too.

◇◇◇◇◇

CHAPTER 27

Did all hospitals smell the same? Like stale air . . . or old fruit?
Like something good gone bad?

The smell stung my nose, bringing back memories, as if
they'd been wrapped up in that scent. Memories of the last
time I went to a hospital, when I was five years old and Mom
had brought me to visit Bubbe. The tubes with clear liquids
going in and dark liquids coming out. The machines with
lights flashing red or green. The plastic breathing tubes going
in her nose.

To me, that smell reminded me of death. And now it was
Zeydeh in that room. Zeydeh lying in that bed.

And it was my fault.

I'd come out to the hospital garden to escape the smell—
and my memories. But I couldn't. It seemed like forever since
Zeydeh collapsed, but it had only been two hours. Dad called
the paramedics and they were there in minutes. A concussion

from the fall, they thought, possibly a fractured arm. Low blood pressure the likely cause of his fainting.

I kept waiting for Zeydeh to open his eyes, but he didn't, not in all the time it took to get him on a stretcher and out to the ambulance. Mom rode with him to the hospital, and he came to for a few seconds, but he didn't seem to know her.

He was awake now, but not really awake. Benny and I got to see him for a few minutes. He had an IV sticking from his hand with a long tube feeding him liquids. His left arm was wrapped in a splint and an ice pack rested against his head. He looked tiny in the bed, like a lumpy pile of sticks.

His eyes were open, but it was as if he were looking into his own mind. "Is the train coming?" His eyes fluttered.

"No, Dad, there's no train," Mom said gently. "Ellie and Benny are here."

"The train is coming," he mumbled. Then his eyes fluttered closed.

"It's okay," Mom told us. "He's not really awake."

But she hadn't looked like it was okay.

Then they'd taken him for tests. Dr. Straus, Zeydeh's doctor, had come by. A concussion, he said. The CAT scan showed a subdural hematoma—a bruise on the brain. They'd monitor it closely. As long as it didn't worsen . . . They'd keep him overnight and see how he was in the morning. Yes, confusion was normal. Try not to worry.

But I was worried. Mom was, too. Dad pretended to be strong, but his eyes were more red than Mom's. Benny didn't say much. He had his iPod on, but I could tell it wasn't very loud, because every time the door leading to the patient rooms opened, he looked up.

The nurses were setting up a reclining chair for Mom in Zeydeh's room. Dad said he'd take us home as soon as we had word about Zeydeh's arm. But the waiting room just made waiting worse. At least the courtyard garden was empty. Even at 8:00 p.m., it was still too warm for most people to want to be outside.

I remembered I'd been to the garden before, too. There were bushes and flower beds and a few trees with twisted green trunks. A flagstone path wound around the garden and through the middle where curved benches faced a fountain. Zeydeh and I had come out here and stood by the fountain. Back then, it had been taller than me. Water poured from a spout at the top, into a wavy-edged bowl, then into another, and finally into a shallow pool. The bottom looked like solid metal from the coins that had been dropped in. I thought of all the people who had tossed in those coins. People like me, praying, hoping. Had their prayers been answered, I wondered?

Zeydeh hadn't dropped in a coin. "What does God need with money?" But he'd stood out here for a long time, staring at the fountain and holding my hand.

I looked into the sky. The hospital lights shone from every floor, a stairway of lights rising where—to heaven? No, not for Zeydeh. *Not for Zeydeh!* I blinked into the shadows, searching beyond what I could see. I squeezed my eyes shut, and my throat closed on a sob.

◇◇◇◇◇

He can't die, God! You can't let him! Hot tears dripped down my cheeks. *It's not his fault—none of this is. Don't make him die. Not because of me. Zeydeh was right: I didn't belong at that camp. I never should have gone. If I hadn't, none of this would have happened. He'd be home right now, making his soup.*

"Ellie?"

I startled and spun around. The electric doors had slid open; I hadn't even heard. Devon stood in the doorway, as if he couldn't decide if he was coming or going. Hurriedly, I wiped my face with the back of my hand. "What are you doing here?"

He stepped out, and the doors swooshed shut behind him. He walked toward me wearing a white polo over jeans. I realized I'd never seen him in jeans before. He looked really good, which for some reason made me feel worse.

"When you didn't show for the performance tonight, I got worried," he said. "I tried calling, but you didn't answer. Finally, Megan got through to your brother, and she told me what happened. How is he?" He reached for my hand, but I folded my arms across my middle.

"I don't know. He has a concussion."

"Your brother said he fainted?"

"I thought he was dead." My voice caught and I turned around to face the fountain. A pebble had gotten stuck in one of the wavy edges. The water swerved and dodged, trying to find a way around the block.

"He'll be okay, Ellie."

I watched a little pool of water gather behind the pebble.

"We had a fight, Devon. A terrible fight. We argue all the time, but not like that. Never like that." I squeezed my eyes shut, trying to block out the memory of what I'd said. If only I could go back. Take it all back.

I opened my eyes and took a careful breath. "Today at camp, he realized I was trying to hide him. My grandpa, who I'm so proud of, and I wanted him to disappear." My voice crumbled into a million pieces, and I went on in a sob. "When I showed up to get him tonight, he was dressed like an Orthodox rabbi. He wanted to out me to your grandmother. And instead of getting mad at *her*, I got mad at him."

"Ellie," he said. I heard the worry in his voice and saw the shadow of his hand reaching out to me. "It's not your fault."

I flinched from his touch. "Then whose fault is it?" I swung to face him, anger rising inside me, turning my tears into acid. "Your grandmother is the racist. Is it her fault?"

"Don't say that."

I lifted my chin, daring him to meet my eyes. "It's true, isn't it? You can call it something else, but that's what it is."

He turned away and stared at the fountain. I could tell he was trying to calm himself. But I didn't want him to be calm. Zeydeh was fighting for his life—how dare Devon be calm!

"I didn't come to argue, Ellie. I just wanted to be with you."

"Well, maybe I don't want to be with you."

The trickling water sounded loud in the sudden quiet. I could see his throat working, but then he hunched his shoulders in a shrug. "Okay. Sorry. I just . . ." His eyes flickered over my face and he swallowed his words. "I'll see you Monday at camp, okay?"

"I won't be at camp on Monday."

"Oh. Oh, right," he stammered. "You'll want to be with your grandpa. I'll tell Grandmother. She'll understand. Even if you don't do your oratory, she'll understand."

"How sweet," I said, my voice dripping sarcasm. "Will she understand when she finds out I'm Jewish?"

"Half Jewish."

"Why do you always say that?" I demanded. "Does that make it okay for you? What if I was one hundred percent Jewish, then what?" I planted my hands on my hips. "Or is your grandmother not the only anti-Semitic person in your family?"

"What?" he gasped. "You're the one who talked about being half and half."

"Maybe there is no half and half. In Nazi Germany there wasn't. I'd have died in a concentration camp for being 'half and half.'"

He gestured with a hand. "This isn't World War II."

I almost laughed. That was my line. How many times had I said that to Zeydeh? "You're right, Devon, it's not. Which is why I shouldn't have had to lie."

He shoved a hand through his hair, gripping his scalp with obvious frustration. "You're the one who wanted the scholarship. I just told you things to help."

"You said it was no big deal."

"I didn't think it was."

190
◇◇◇◇◇

"Well, it is!" My voice cracked, and I swallowed hard. "Why couldn't you have stood up for me?"

He held up his hands. "What was I supposed to do?"

"I don't know," I cried. "Maybe you could have told your grandmother your girlfriend is Jewish and to get over herself."

"Ellie—"

"Forget it." I cut off the excuse I could hear coming. "How could I expect you to stand up for me when you won't even stand up for yourself?"

His jaw pulsed. "What does that mean?"

"You know what it means. You just follow along, do whatever they tell you."

"You could have spoken up, too, you know." Now he looked as mad as I felt. "But you wanted the money."

His words stung. Because they were true.

"Not anymore," I said, my voice feeling raw. "I wouldn't take a dime from your grandmother."

He paused. "What about Benedict's?"

I glanced up toward the line of windows. In one of those lit rooms, Zeydeh was lying in a bed. "My grandpa wanted me to tell your grandmother the truth," I said, "and I'm going to. Then, I'm done with it all. Benedict's. The scholarship."

You.

I couldn't say it out loud. Instead, I whispered, "All of it."

His eyes were dark shadows—for once they were almost black and ugly. "Fine. I won't bother arguing." His voice was full of sarcasm. "It's not like I stand up for myself, anyway." Then he backed toward the hospital doors. "If you have

191

something to say to my grandmother, great." He stepped on the rubber mat in front of the door, tripping the automatic sensors. The glass doors slid open. Lights spilled from the lobby, shadowing a figure as it moved toward the opening. Then she stepped outside.

"You can tell her now," Devon said. "She's the one who drove me here." He turned and walked back inside, leaving me alone with the night and Doris Yeats.

CHAPTER 28

"Hello, Ellie," she said. Her expression oozed concern. "How is your grandfather?"

"I'm not sure," I said. "He's still with the doctors."

Her heels clicked on the flagstone as she stepped farther into the garden. "I can only imagine how worried you must be. Devon was beside himself when I stopped at Benedict's tonight. He just had to see you." She wore a peach skirt and a dressy white blouse that shimmered like crystals of snow. While I'd been fighting with Zeydeh, she'd been at a party.

"Can I do anything for you or your family?" she asked.

I shook my head. "I just need to tell you something. About my grandpa." Now that the moment was here, I couldn't work up even a little fear over this conversation. I just wanted it over.

"Of course," she said.

I wove my fingers through my hair and tucked it behind

my ears. "You once asked me about him, remember? You asked me his name."

She nodded.

"I told you it was Samuel Morris. But that was only half of it. His whole name is Samuel Morris Levine." I raised my chin. "I didn't tell you because he's Jewish. Because I'm Jewish. It wasn't all a total lie," I couldn't help adding. "My dad was raised Lutheran. But I was raised Jewish."

Her blue eyes had turned darker than the sky.

It didn't matter. I was almost done. "I did it because I wanted the scholarship, and Devon said I'd have a better chance if you only knew the Lutheran half."

Her throat worked up and down, but she didn't say anything.

"Anyway." I shrugged. "I'm pulling my application for the scholarship. I don't want it anymore."

I steeled myself for her to get mad or mean or both. But instead she took a step closer. Light circled her hair like a silver halo. "If that's how you feel," she said softly. "But for the record, I already knew you were Jewish. In fact, it's one of the reasons I wanted you to have the scholarship."

I must have looked ready to faint, because she gestured to the cement bench. "Why don't we sit down?"

She sat on one end, crossing her legs and smoothing her skirt over her knees. I sat on the other end, knock-kneed and gripping the bench for balance. "I don't understand."

She looked toward the lit entrance to the hospital. "This

really isn't the place, but perhaps now is as good a time as any." She smiled gently. "First of all, Ellie, I'm not a racist."

My grip loosened, along with my stomach muscles. I felt like I could take a full breath for the first time in days.

"Racism is ignorance. I hope you'll agree I'm not an ignorant person."

"I know that."

"I grew up with Jews, Ellie." She smiled comfortingly. "I speak from experience. They're truly not like the rest of us, and they don't want to be."

An icy shiver shot through me, freezing my breath. I heard the words, but I couldn't make sense of them.

"You're young and naive," she said, "and you've been filled with stories. Of course, you're confused. What I'm saying to you now you'll need to think about. I understand that. I want you to know I understand a lot of things. I've been watching you," she added. "I think you're starting to see there's more in this world. There's a greater truth. Another path."

I clutched the bench harder. It was still warm from the sun and the heat felt good against my numb fingers. If only I could figure out the soft smile, the kind voice.

"You and I are a lot alike, Ellie. In fact, I see myself in you." Her smile widened. "I was also a competitor. A hard worker. I didn't grow up wealthy, but I was determined. We're similar in other ways, as well. You and I are both strong enough to know ourselves. To be honest with ourselves."

When would this start making sense?

"There's a reason you wrote 'Christian' on that application. I think it was a cry from deep within yourself. Maybe not consciously done, but nonetheless."

I gasped, words finally coming from my cold lips. "You think I want to be Christian?"

She smiled as if she knew more than I did. "Your mother's phone call only confirmed it."

Confusion spun through me. I felt dizzy. "What do you mean, my mother's phone call?"

"The message she left, informing me quite clearly of your Jewish background."

"You said you didn't get the message." I remembered Devon hinting that something wasn't right. But it hadn't made sense for her to lie. It still didn't.

"I admit, I was angry at first. But I'd seen you in church just the previous day," she went on. "I watched you pray, Ellie. I could feel there was a connection for you. It started to make sense."

"No. You don't understand. I was just trying to fit in! For the scholarship."

Diamond earrings flashed like prisms as she tilted her head. "Perhaps that's how it began. But I wonder if that's all it really is. I've seen the way you and Devon connect. The way you've fit in so well with the group from Benedict's. You didn't just keep your faith secret from me. You kept it from your classmates and your teacher. Believe me, I understand. Why would you want to identify yourself as one of those people?"

I shook my head in disbelief. "You're just saying that

196

because of a bad business deal with someone Jewish. Devon told me."

She smiled a little. "Is that what he said?"

"But my family is really nice," I said. "If you got to know them—my grandpa is terrible at business. He can't even balance his checkbook. My dad has to do it."

Her smooth hand squeezed mine. "It's very sweet, Ellie, your defending your family. I commend you for it. But you cannot defend an entire race. Certainly not to me," she added. "I know exactly what they're like. Arrogant and self-important. Wrapping themselves in the mantle of 'the chosen people.'" Her eyes narrowed as if she were seeing a long way off.

I rubbed the ache at my temples. "I don't understand why you say things like that. Why you think that way."

She studied me for so long, I had to look down. "You think I'm being unfair, don't you? You might be surprised, Ellie." Her lips twitched with the hint of a smile. "Yes, I think you might be very surprised."

"About what?"

"About the fact that once, a very long time ago, I fancied myself in love with a Jew."

I gaped in surprise. "You were in love?"

"I imagined myself so," she said with a nod. "As young girls will." She laughed as if it was funny, but there was nothing funny about the intense look in her eyes. Goose bumps prickled on my bare arms.

"He was a boy I met in college," she explained. "A Jewish

boy. I ignored my natural apprehensions and allowed myself to become involved. We even talked of an engagement."

"He broke it off?" I guessed, my voice barely louder than a whisper.

She looked at me, her eyes sparking blue fire. "Certainly not. He was very much in love. It was his parents who opposed the relationship. They didn't consider me suitable," she said with icy precision. "Can you imagine? No shiksa was good enough for their son. You must know that word, Ellie. As a non-Jew, I was unacceptable." She laughed again, a harsh sound that felt like sandpaper over my skin.

"I'm so sorry."

"Do not. Be. Sorry," she snapped. "On the contrary." She paused, and I could see her take a long, deep breath. Her voice level again, she said, "I owe them a great debt of thanks for opening my eyes. And it has been one of the pleasures of my life to know I've succeeded in every way beyond that family."

"But that was just one family," I said. "And they were wrong."

"No, they were right," she corrected. "They belong with their own kind. Just as we belong with ours."

They? We? Ours?

A hospital helicopter flew over us. The noise roared in my head like a living thing. I covered my ears, but the confusion was inside me.

Their kind. Our kind.

What kind was I?

The helicopter faded, and I think Mrs. Yeats said more, but

I wasn't sure what. Then she reached for my hand again. "I want to help you. If you attend Benedict's, I know I can."

She pressed her hand over mine, waiting for me to say something, but I couldn't think what to say. I couldn't think.

She seemed to understand. "There's no need for you to say anything right now." She stood up, her expression full of understanding. "It's a lot to take in, and especially when you're terribly worried about your grandfather, as you should be. I'll pray for his health. And for you."

I closed my eyes. Wished I could escape into the blackness behind my lids. But her voice flowed around me. Through me.

"Don't worry about camp this week. Assuming your grandfather is recovered sufficiently, I'll see you Thursday night for the oratory final. I realize your speech won't be polished, but I don't want you to worry about that. You understand?" She paused. "Your performance is only a formality, Ellie. The scholarship is yours."

CHAPTER 29

"I brought you a stale cinnamon roll and a Coke," Megan said. "It's regular. I figured you could use extra sugar with your caffeine."

Megan had shown up a while ago—I wasn't sure how long. Or even what time it was. She'd taken one look at me and prescribed immediate sugar. "Here," she said, handing me the goodies. I took the bottle of Coke and shook my head at the bag. I couldn't eat.

She sat down next to me.

I held the Coke to my forehead for a second, rolling the cold plastic on my skin. "You were gone awhile," I said. "Any news?"

"I'm supposed to tell you Zeydeh is finally back from x-ray. He's got a broken humerus—the upper bone in his arm—but it's a clean break and the doctor thinks it'll heal like new."

I stood. "I'll go up."

"Hang on," she said, grabbing my arm. "He's getting a cast

put on. Your mom says wait a little while and then you can see him."

I sat back down.

"Maybe you should fix yourself up before you see Zeydeh. You look like two faucets broke and soaked your face."

"Thanks." I took a drink. The bubbles fizzed down my throat and felt good in my empty stomach.

"Your brother said Devon showed up a while ago."

I nodded. "Guess who drove him here? Dear old Granny."

"Uh-oh."

"Yeah," I agreed. "We had a real nice heart-to-heart."

"Is she up in a room with a dented gluteus maximus?"

"I *should* have kicked her butt," I muttered. I took another swallow of Coke. "I told her I'm Jewish."

Megan sighed. She leaned close and bumped my shoulder. "You know, I've been thinking. Benedict's is completely lame. I'm going to Canyon View with you."

"She says the scholarship is still mine."

"What?" Megan jumped to her feet. "No way!" She startled two birds I hadn't known were in a tree.

"Not so fast. There's more."

Megan dropped back down. "Why is there always more?"

"She said she's not a racist. Basically, because she's right about Jews."

"Okay," she said, jumping up again. "*I'm* going to kick her butt."

I pulled her back down. "I know. It's sick. But then . . ." I sighed. "It was weird, Meg. She told me how she was in love with a Jewish guy in college, only his parents didn't approve of her. They made him break it off because she *wasn't* Jewish."

"Serious?"

I nodded. "I almost felt sorry for her."

"And Devon never told you about that?"

"I don't think he knows. I got the feeling she doesn't talk about it much."

"But she told you?"

"Maybe so I'd understand."

"What?" Megan asked.

"I don't know. That she has a good reason."

"To hate you?" Megan's eyebrows lifted so high, they cleared the top of her glasses. "Maybe she has reason to hate that guy's parents. I mean, that was like reverse anti-Semitism or something."

"I know."

"But still," she said. "It's like me hating all fruits just because strawberries give me hives."

I frowned. "Huh?"

Megan waved her hand in the air. "Don't think about it too long. I'm terrible with analogies. The point is, it's stupid to hate millions of people because of one bad apple."

"Is this another fruit analogy?"

She laughed. "You know what I mean."

"Yeah. I do." And I felt a lot better. Maybe what happened to Mrs. Yeats had been crappy, but it wasn't a reason to hate a whole religion.

Or to try and make me hate it, too.

I gave Megan a look. "That wasn't all she said."

She groaned. "I'm afraid to ask."

"She said she can tell that I don't like Jews either. That it's obvious I chose not to be one of the chosen people."

"Huh?"

"I filled out the application saying I'm Christian and she says that's a sign." I reached to my throat where Bubbe's necklace should have been hanging. "She doesn't know about my Jewish star, but she'd say that's a sign, too." I fought the sudden pressure behind my eyes. "But it's not, is it?"

"Of course it's not," Megan agreed.

I couldn't stop my mind from going back to this afternoon—to Zeydeh in the Benedict's lobby. How embarrassed I'd been. How I'd tried to hurry him out. And then the fight. Pictures of it flashed in my mind like an evil PowerPoint. I wasn't trying to be someone else. I just wanted to get into Benedict's. Doris Yeats was wrong. Completely wrong.

"I say stuff all the time I don't actually believe."

Megan nodded. "Everyone does."

"Remember Regionals last year when I argued for school uniforms?"

"You were awesome."

"But that didn't mean I wanted to wear one."

"Who would?" Megan asked. "Anything that has to fit five hundred different people cannot be attractive. It was just a position."

"That's what I was doing at camp. My goal was the scholarship. I looked at all sides, found an angle, and went for it."

"Exactly."

The traitorous slide show in my head replayed the beginning of camp. "Maybe I did do some bad stuff," I admitted. *Hiding the necklace. Accepting Devon's lame explanation. Praying with everyone like I was one of them. Swaying and humming to the Lord's Prayer. Going to church. Lying about Zeydeh's name.*

"You did what anyone else would have done. Look at me." Megan held up her arms. "Is this the real me?"

She gave me a little smile and I noticed the red lips outlined in black. Preeba lips. She wore the net stockings and a leopard-print shirt with fake fur, and she had a sparkling red tattoo of a broken heart on her neck. Angry Goth with a touch of playful. I sat up straight, suddenly remembering. "I can't believe I forgot to ask. How did it go tonight?"

She shrugged, but I could see her cheeks pinken. "Our scene took first place."

"Serious?" I reached over and hugged her, smelling the fresh lemon that Megan had slid over her wrists as part of her Preeba persona. She felt so solid under the polyester and fake fur. "Oh, Megan, that's awesome! I knew you would."

"Anna's scene took second, but she was incredible."

I pulled back. "Second? I wish I'd been there to see you guys. Your mom and dad must have been thrilled."

She nodded. "My mom gave me a standing O. I think she likes me better as Preeba."

"You've got to cut her some slack."

She adjusted the strip of fur around her neck. "Why should I? It's the truth. If she could reinvent me, she would."

"She loves you."

"Not the real me."

"Maybe if you gave her a chance."

"She had a chance," Megan shot back, her eyes like lasers behind her glasses. "She wanted to dress me up like Barbie and take me to cotillion events. Those things are not *me*."

"And Preeba is?"

She rolled her eyes.

And suddenly it hit me what she was saying. I was trying to be someone else so I could fit in, while Megan was trying to be someone else so she didn't fit in. How screwed up was that?

Megan squeezed my arm. "The important thing right now is you. What are you going to do?"

"Mrs. Yeats said all I have to do is show up and give my oratory, and the scholarship is mine. As if I'd still want it."

As if I'd still want Benedict's. And the speech team.

And Devon.

My tear ducts filled. Again. My head throbbed. I felt sick, like I'd eaten something bad. Only it wasn't food—it was me that was bad. A part of me.

Because I did want those things.

Still.

My heart sank under the weight of guilt. I couldn't go back to camp. I couldn't give my oratory. I couldn't take the scholarship.

I couldn't let Mrs. Yeats be right about me.

CHAPTER 30

"Ellie, tell this crazy woman I have to go home!"

Zeydeh shouted his order at me as soon as I walked in. The crazy woman was my mother, who didn't look worried this morning. She looked pissed.

Suddenly, the sun coming in from the tiny window seemed brighter. The hospital room didn't even smell so bad today—probably because Dad had filled a water bucket with mixed flowers, and the room smelled like something living instead of something dying.

And, Zeydeh wasn't dying. Though, come to think of it, Mom looked ready to kill him.

"You can't get out of this bed. Do you want to faint again?"

"Faint, schmaint. I have soup to make," Zeydeh said.

Mom rolled her eyes and blew out a breath. "You see how he's been?" she said to me. "Where's your father?"

"Cafeteria with Benny."

She ran a hand over her face, pushing her hair off her forehead. Dad had come back last night with an overnight bag for Mom. The green dress with the repaired zipper was now stuffed into the gray duffel, and Mom wore a long-sleeve T-shirt, baggy black sweats, and flip-flops.

"I'm going to go grab a coffee. Maybe you can talk some sense into him, Ellie. He seems to think a pot of soup is more important than his health."

She leaned over and kissed his forehead. "Try not to do anything stupid for the five minutes I'm gone."

She gave me a quick kiss on the cheek, then walked out.

I smiled, blinking back an urge to cry. It was stupid to cry now—he was doing so much better. I grabbed the metal bed rail, looking him up and down. "So you're okay?"

He lay in bed, a green gown tied loosely over his shoulders, and the blankets pulled up to his chest. His skin looked pale, even with a clean white bandage tied around his head, but his eyes were full of fire.

"Of course I'm okay. It was nothing. A bump on the head." He looked me up and down. "You look like *farkakte*."

"You're not one to talk," I retorted. A long tube ran from a bag of liquid and into a needle stuck in the back of his hand, where the skin had bruised into a quilt of black and blue.

"It's only an IV," he said, following my gaze. "For fluids."

I swallowed thickly. "I should have paid more attention. You weren't drinking your juice. You weren't taking care of yourself."

"You can't take credit for my stupidity, Ellie."

◇◇◇◇◇

Before I could stop them, tears started dripping down my cheeks.

His face smoothed and softened. He patted the side of his bed. "Come sit. And stop with the tears. With all this equipment, you'll electrocute us." He winked, then grimaced. "Oy," he moaned. "My head feels like a lump of dough someone's kneaded too long." He gestured toward the bandage. "How do I look with my head all wrapped up?"

"Like a gift." I sat on the edge of the bed, careful not to bump him.

He smiled. "It's just to keep an ice pack on; don't look so scared. My head is still in one piece. They'll have to make a stronger floor to put a dent in Samuel Levine's head."

New tears pooled in the corner of my eyes. "I'm so sorry, Zeydeh."

"It takes two to argue." He tried to sound gruff but already his voice sounded weaker—he was tiring out. "Help me up a little," he said. "This bed has more humps than a herd of camels." He held my hand and I helped him slide up a few inches.

"You were right about camp and Benedict's and everything," I said. "I want you to know I'm done with it. All of it. What matters now is getting you better."

"Nonsense," he said. He wanted to wave me off but couldn't. One hand was stuck with an IV; the other arm was wrapped to the wrist in a cast. "My head is pounding too much for such grand gestures."

"Should I call the nurse?" I reached for the nurse's button that hung by the bed.

He stopped me with a frown. "It's nothing that can't be cured by going home." He blinked at me. His eyes looked so old and tired. "I need to get home, Ellie. There's a chicken in the refrigerator. I need to clean it and season it. I need to start the soup."

"But your arm, Zeydeh."

"I'll manage with one arm."

"You heard Mom. You're not strong enough."

"And what is the best cure, Ellie? What is the world's best medicine?"

I smiled, knowing the answer. "Chicken soup."

"You've got to get me out of here," he said. "Today is Saturday. Tomorrow is the cooking contest. If I go home now, there's still time. I can still have my soup ready." There was a glint of panic in his eyes I'd never seen before. "Ellie," he said, his voice trembling, "you must help me get home."

In the end, it wasn't until Sunday morning that Zeydeh was released from the hospital. He spiked a fever on Saturday, and the doctor insisted he stay another night for observation. Mom threatened to sit on him when he tried to get up on his own.

The soup, she said, would have to wait one more year. I couldn't repeat what Zeydeh said back. I'd never even heard half the cuss words, but I knew they must be bad ones.

It wasn't that Mom didn't feel terrible. We both did. But

neither one of us knew how to stew a chicken and add the right herbs—not to Zeydeh's standards. And it had to be done Saturday night so the cooked chicken could sit overnight in the fridge. Otherwise, Zeydeh said, the flavors would never come alive and the soup would lie on the tongue like a dead thing. I paced the hospital hallways for hours, wishing there was something I could do.

Then it came to me. Maybe there was. I ran to the cafeteria and found Mom and Dad sharing a stale donut. "I have an idea," I said.

Mom's eyes brightened when I told them. She grinned at Dad. "I love it."

"I love it, too," Dad agreed. "But Zeydeh is going to hate it."

◇

We brought him home on Sunday in the VW. The sun was bright overhead with nothing but a few puffy clouds to break up the blue sky. Zeydeh grumbled the whole way and the rest of us tried not to listen. If he hadn't been so glum, he might have noticed all the smiles we shot each other.

Dad and Benny got Zeydeh's overnight bag and all the medical supplies from the back. Mom went ahead to open the door, and I walked Zeydeh up the sidewalk. "Careful," I said. "There's a step."

He rolled his eyes. "I've lived here almost ten years. You think I've forgotten the step?"

Mom pushed open the door and moved aside, making room

for Zeydeh. He stopped at the doorway. His nose wrinkled. "What's that I smell?" He looked from Mom to me. "Did I leave soup on the stove?"

I raised my eyebrows as if I were surprised. "Why don't you go see?"

He glared, but there was more energy in his step as he hurried into the hall. Then he stopped, nearly backing into me. An elderly woman with silver hair, wide brown eyes, and bright red lipstick sat in one of the chairs facing the door.

"Mrs. Zuckerman?" he whispered, astonished.

Her lips twitched. "You were expecting Moses?"

I swallowed a laugh, but Zeydeh didn't look amused.

"What are you doing in here?" he demanded.

"Making your soup," she retorted. "What else?"

"My soup?"

"From the notes you left—not that your handwriting is anything to be proud of."

"You made my soup?" he repeated.

"Only to stew the chicken last night." She smiled softly then, her eyes getting all drippy, and I realized Mrs. Zuckerman had a thing for my zeydeh. It was kind of sweet. Only, it suddenly made me think of Devon with a sharp pang. He was never going to look at me like that now. We were never going to have a thing for each other. We were the antithing. We were nothing. I wished the thought of it would stop hurting already.

Zeydeh looked helplessly at the sling keeping his left arm immobile. "But my arm."

"So I'll wash up. You'll tell me what to do next." As if she'd lived there all her life, she stood up and walked back to the kitchen. A second later we heard the faucet running.

"You did this?" he said to me.

"You're not mad, are you?"

I could see it was finally sinking in. "You called Mrs. Zuckerman, the spy?"

"She's not a spy. She's a very nice lady."

"*Hoomf*," he grumbled. He glared in the direction of the kitchen. "She's very bossy. Did you hear her? Complaining about my handwriting?" But he shuffled toward the kitchen with his shoulders back. "You know how to make a matzo ball?" he asked her.

"What do you think?" she said. "I was born yesterday?"

"A soft touch is what it takes."

"Soft as the skin on a baby's bottom."

"*Hoomf.*"

Mom and I exchanged smiles. Dad and Benny set down Zeydeh's stuff.

"How's it going?" Dad whispered.

Mom gestured to the kitchen and we all stood there, listening.

"You added the onions and the celery?" Zeydeh demanded. "The herbs and seasonings, just as I had them written?"

"Of course," she said, impatience in her voice. "I'd never use so much pepper myself."

I heard the silverware drawer open, then the sound of a slurp. "Not bad," Zeydeh said.

"Not bad? That's better than not bad! Even if it is your recipe."

We all smiled at each other.

"Should we leave them to it?" Dad asked.

"We'll be back in a couple of hours," Mom called out. "In time to load everything up and take it to the synagogue."

Zeydeh didn't bother answering. Something was cooking in the kitchen. I had a feeling it was more than matzo ball soup.

CHAPTER 31

"Such a day," Zeydeh said, yawning.

He looked as exhausted as he sounded. His eyes were half open, as if he didn't have the energy to lift his eyelids. His face was pale under a layer of stubble, his jaw slack, and his shoulders slumped under the white T-shirt he wore to bed. But every few seconds his lips twitched in a half smile, and I knew he was going back over the day.

The Har Zion Synagogue Cooking Contest had officially begun at three o'clock that afternoon, and Zeydeh had managed to finish his pot of soup in time. For a while, it had looked dicey. Zeydeh and Mrs. Zuckerman got in an argument over whether to transport the soup in the cooking pot or in a Crock-Pot, and almost made us late. In the end, Zeydeh put his foot down, said it was his soup, and he was taking it in the cooking pot.

Mrs. Zuckerman gave in gracefully. She never even said a

word when Zeydeh realized the soup wouldn't stay hot long enough for all the judging, and decided (last minute) to transfer it to a Crock-Pot.

Mrs. Zuckerman made a platter of chopped liver paté, which Zeydeh said needed more pepper. I thought it tasted amazing—especially when you considered she started with the internal organs of a chicken. As nervous as Zeydeh was during the judging, I knew he secretly thought it was amazing, too. There were twelve entries total, but he worried most about Mrs. Zuckerman's, hovering around the tables as the judges took their tastes, trying to read their faces, and working himself into a state of panic.

Mom got him to sit down for an hour while the judges made their decision. After all, he'd only just been released from the hospital that morning. It was too much for him, she warned. But I think even Mom admitted it was all worth it when the winner was announced.

"Shmuel ben Yakov," the rabbi said, looking through half glasses at the index card with the judges' final results. "Samuel Morris Levine, for his matzo ball soup."

Zeydeh was so thrilled, he kissed us all on both cheeks, then led Mrs. Zuckerman in a dance until they were both breathless. Mrs. Zuckerman took second prize, but didn't seem to mind. She kept an eye on Zeydeh through the whole thing. It was kind of sweet. I'd never thought of him with anyone but Bubbe, but watching him dance made me realize how lonely he must be.

"I like Mrs. Zuckerman," I said to him now.

He bobbed his head side to side. "She's very bossy."

"You could use someone bossy."

"For that I have you and your mother." His lips twitched again.

"But she's coming over in the morning?"

"For coffee and a pomegranate-and-prune muffin."

I laughed. "She must really like you if she's willing to eat one of those."

He gargled low in his throat as if I were ridiculous, but that smile was there again.

I slid to the edge of my chair so I could pat his knee. "You need to go to bed, Zeydeh."

"I'm too happy to sleep." He yawned. "When did they say the plaque would be engraved?"

"By Tuesday," I said.

"Is it Tuesday yet?"

"It's still Sunday, Zeydeh. It's three hours since you won."

"Who won?" he asked, that half smile playing around his lips.

I laughed. "You won."

He grinned, his eyes all but closed. At least I'd gotten him settled into his favorite padded chair with a soft afghan spread over his lap and legs. Mom, Dad, and Benny had gone home, but Zeydeh had asked me to stay.

"If you won't go to sleep," I said, "can I ask a question?"

"Will I know the answer?"

"I hope so. Because I want to know why it was so important for you to win this. You said you wanted your name on a plaque but . . . why?"

His lids lifted and the fuzzy blue eyes were suddenly awake. "That's quite a question."

"You were so worried this year."

"Maybe because I have fewer years to worry."

I reached for his right hand. "Don't say that."

His fingers curved around mine and held tight. If only the bones didn't look so fragile.

"It's the truth, Ellie," he said gently. "And when I'm gone, I wonder what the world will remember of Samuel Morris Levine. What kind of name did I make for myself?"

"A good one, Zeydeh. The best." My eyes suddenly felt full.

He took a breath, but I wondered if he heard me. His mind seemed somewhere else. "I've always thought about Bubbe's cousins who died in the concentration camps," he said. "They were young. They had no time to live a life. For many like them, all that is left is a name, engraved on a wall in a museum. So many names. So many Jewish names. All engraved for the wrong reasons—for terrible reasons."

His gaze shifted back to my face. "All my life, I've wanted to have my name engraved for a good reason. In honor of those who had no chance. But a life, no matter how long, is still the blink of an eye. And mine is nearing the end." He smiled. "In all these years, I never saw my name engraved on a plaque. Can you imagine?" He shrugged. "It's a silly thing, I know, but an old man has earned the right to a little silliness, I hope."

"It's not silly," I managed around a lump in my throat.

He shifted on his chair, sitting forward and a little straighter.

◇◇◇◇◇

"In one way or another, we all work to make a name for ourselves, Ellie. You will make a name for yourself, too."

"I will, Zeydeh."

His eyes stared straight into mine, a knowing look in their depths. "This whole weekend you've barely left me. I wonder about your oratory. The tournament is only four days away. Is it written? Is it memorized?"

"I told you. I'm done with camp."

"What? You mean the nonsense you told me at the hospital?" He pulled his hand free to wave it at me in disgust. "You've been upset and worried, but enough is enough, Ellie. You are not meant to be an old man's nurse."

"It's not just that. You were right about the camp, Zeydeh. I didn't belong there. Besides, Canyon View has a great speech program."

"But it won't be Benedict's."

"I can still be a great orator without Benedict's."

"Of course you can. But this is not the way to do it."

"What way?"

"To give up—to quit."

I ran both hands over my forehead and through my bangs. I could suddenly feel how tired I was. I hadn't slept much either in the past couple of days. "I'm not quitting," I said. "You don't understand. In fact, you should be very proud of me."

"For not competing? This you'll have to explain."

I pulled at the edge of his afghan, freeing a snagged thread. "I talked to Mrs. Yeats the other night. She brought Devon to the hospital. She said really crazy things."

"What things?"

"She said I didn't really want to be Jewish. The way I acted proved it. She said I was a lot like her—that she saw so much potential. I shouldn't let being Jewish ruin things for me."

"*Oy vey*," he mumbled.

"Here's the best part. She wants me to have the scholarship. All I have to do is come to the final performance and give my oratory, and it's mine."

"And what will you do?" he asked calmly.

"Nothing!" I lifted my chin. "I'm not going. No way am I giving my oratory."

He scratched at his cheek a long moment. "You could show up and pretend you agree with her. Take her money and go to Benedict's."

"How can you say that?"

"That's what you did before."

My throat squeezed tight. "I was wrong."

"Or was she right, Ellie? The crazy things she said?"

"No!" I shook my head hard enough to make myself dizzy. "I just wanted the scholarship, Zeydeh. Honest."

"Then why have these things she said stayed with you? Why do they matter?"

This time, tears did fill my eyes.

"Be honest, Ellie."

"Because I did want to be like her," I said, my voice trembling. "She's so successful and important. I was proud she picked me out of everyone else. I wanted her to want me." I buried my head in the crook of my elbow, soaking my sleeve with tears. "I still do. What's wrong with me, Zeydeh?"

"Nothing," he said fiercely. "Who in this world doesn't wish to be loved for who they are? You think you're the only one?" I felt shaky fingers slide beneath my chin, and he raised my face. "You think you're the only one to be rejected? Deemed unacceptable?"

I looked at him through blurry eyes. "But how can she believe that?"

"What's important is whether *you* believe it."

"She said I wouldn't have lied unless I secretly want to be a Christian."

"Of course that's what she said. That's what she'd like to believe." He wiped his thumb across my cheek, catching my tears with his touch. "Only you can decide the truth of who you are and who you want to be. Mrs. Yeats does not get to decide. Even I do not get to decide."

He sighed so hard that his shoulders drooped a few inches. "What I tried to do Friday night was wrong. When I dressed up in full Jewish regalia, I wanted to say something—not about me but about you. I wanted to speak for you."

"Because I didn't do it for myself."

"And that is why we were both wrong." The afghan slid off his legs and pooled onto the floor. He didn't seem to notice. "Each of us is unique, Ellie. That is God's greatest gift to us— and his greatest challenge. You must find the courage to speak with your own unique voice. Otherwise, someone else will speak for you. You'll be amazed at how many want the job."

He rolled his eyes with disgust. "Your parents, your friends, your enemies, politicians and teachers—all these voices will try to speak for you. Sometimes, it seems easier to let them. But then, you've lost more than your voice. You've lost yourself."

I peeled back strands of hair from my wet cheeks. "What if I don't hear my own voice?"

"You'll hear it. You just may not want to listen." He patted my knee again. "Whatever you decide, whatever you do, do it because it's what your heart tells you is right." He smiled, and his gaze drifted to the afghan.

"What is it, Zeydeh?"

"I was just thinking about your name. You remember how you hated your name?"

"You try being a fifth grader with a name like Eleanor."

He chuckled. "It's a good name. Eleanor for my grandmother. Jane for your bubbe's cousin. And, of course, Taylor from your father. These names are part of your history; they represent those who came before you. But they are only a foundation. Now the name must grow with you. That is truly a sacred responsibility. You give life to your name, and in the end, only your name lives on."

"I know that's supposed to be inspiring," I said. "But mostly it's pretty scary."

"What do you expect?" He furrowed his curly brows at me. "I am a scary old man. But you're my granddaughter and I love you—whoever you choose to be."

I slid off my seat then and laid my head in his lap. He

221
◇◇◇◇◇

smelled like chicken soup and vanilla and I wanted to bury myself in his lap and hide there forever.

As if he knew what I was thinking, he gently pulled me away with his good arm. "Enough for one night." He smiled to take the sting from his words. "I'm tired and I don't need your help to find my bed. So go, already. Come in the morning. I'll save you a muffin."

Outside, it felt like the world had closed down for the night. Moonlight turned the houses into sleeping shadows and made the asphalt look like a flat sea of gray. Cicadas buzzed in the darkness, and somewhere near my feet, I heard a lizard shoot across the path and into some bushes. I could see the porch light of my house, but I wasn't ready to go home yet. My head was too full of everything Zeydeh had said.

A month ago, I knew exactly who I was. I was the girl who was going to win a scholarship and be someone. How did everything get so screwed up?

How did I get so screwed up?

Alone with only the soft slap of my sandals on the sidewalk, I had to be honest with myself. It wasn't just the scholarship and the speech team. It was Devon. It was the amazing campus and being accepted by the Benedict's kids. It was my whole stupid idea of how great it would all be. How great I would be. I'd pretty much convinced myself I was so perfect, how could Mrs. Yeats *not* like me?

No way could she *hate* me.

Even now, the thought of it made my stomach churn. Nobody had ever hated me before. But now I knew I could be hated—and not just by one woman. By thousands and thousands of people. They'd never even met me and they hated me. There could be people, right now, looking up at the same stars and wishing me dead. Wishing people like me dead. Jewish people.

I stopped on the edge of our front lawn and wrapped my arms across my waist, trembling in the warm night. Did that make me want to stop being Jewish? To change who I was?

I gazed at the sky, trying to see beyond the dark purplish blue. You could look and look and not feel like you were seeing anything. If I stared long enough, would I start to see? Would God show me a sign? I closed my eyes and thought about all that hate.

Did it make me want to change?

The truth went through me like a whisper. Like a breath from the past.

No.

It was as if I were suddenly surrounded by ghosts—the ghosts of Bubbe and her family, of my great-grandmother Eleanor and her family. I wasn't the first . . . I wasn't alone.

No.

It felt good to think it, to feel it. I was me. I was Eleanor Jane Taylor. I was my zeydeh's granddaughter and I had guts. No, correct that: I had chutzpah—the Jewish equivalent of guts. Because I was Jewish. And knowing some people might hate me because of it didn't make me want to change.

It made me want to change *them!*

The realization buzzed through me like a shot of

carbonation to my blood. My fingers tingled . . . everything tingled. Even my hair felt electric and alive. This was it. The thing I was meant to do. I'd told Devon I wanted to change people's minds about something important, and this was my chance.

Starting with Mrs. Yeats.

But how? The thought brought my head out of the clouds. If I showed up and gave my oratory, she would say it only proved she was right. But if I didn't show up, why would she listen to me ever again? And I had to make her listen.

Unless . . . A crazy idea swirled through my head. A way to prove myself and guarantee she listened. My heart thumped. If I could make Mrs. Yeats understand, then I really could have everything. But I only had four days; it wasn't enough time to do it right. I'd be crazy to even try. I half smiled to myself. As crazy as my zeydeh.

I sprinted toward the front door. Suddenly, I was too nervous to be tired. For the first time, I'd be arguing for something I really believed in. Me.

CHAPTER 32

The stage curtains were drawn, and the overhead lights in the auditorium were dimmed. Spotlights lit the center of the stage like a full moon in a dark sky. A podium had been centered for those who wanted to use it, with a microphone attached. Andrew stood under the glare of lights, trying to look relaxed. Those first few minutes when you stood there waiting for the judges to give you the nod—those were the hardest.

This was it, our final tourney. Tomorrow was Friday, the last day of camp, when the Benedict's Scholarship would be announced. I sat in the dark, in the front row, with the rest of my class. Sarah nervously twisted her hair on my right, and I could hear Ethan popping his retainer in and out on my left. It wasn't as if I'd purposely sat as far from Devon as I could, but I wondered if he had. Tonight was the first time I'd seen him since the hospital, since I'd blamed him for everything and told him to go away. How could I blame him for wanting to avoid me now?

He didn't look like he'd lost any sleep over it. He still looked so good it made my stomach hurt. He wore a deep blue suit and a pink shirt the color of Pepto-Bismol—and he still managed to look hot. From now on, I was only falling for ugly guys. It was so much easier when you broke up.

I knew I had to face him, but I couldn't do it now. Not before I spoke. After I'd finished . . . well, I guess we'd see.

Andrew worked his way through a speech on why our society was so fixated on winning—kind of ironic, since he was trying to win. It was the best thing I'd seen him do all month, though. Sarah nailed her oratory on the loss of personal communication in a high-tech world. When Devon took the stage, I could hardly breathe. It felt like that first day of camp when I looked into his eyes and blanked on the topic. He dove into the intro and I smiled, remembering every word because we'd worked on it together. But then he transitioned into the main body, and it was like he had moved away from me. Moved on. Like none of it had ever happened.

My head felt dizzy. Had it all been a dream, Devon and me? I looked at my hands curled in my lap. He'd held my hand and squeezed my fingers and I'd felt goose bumps up my spine every single time. I rubbed one hand over the other, as if I could still feel the imprint of Devon's hand. As if I could prove to myself that it had been real.

The audience was still clapping when Mrs. Clancy stepped

back to the podium and leaned toward the mic. "Our next orator will be Ellie Taylor."

My lungs squeezed at the sound of my name.

This is it.

I slipped off the jacket I'd been wearing, trying not to feel half naked. I lifted the black canvas bag with the last piece of my outfit and walked to the stage steps, careful not to wobble on my high heels. Behind me, two rows back, I could hear my cheering section: Mom, Dad, Benny, and Zeydeh, plus Megan and her parents.

But Mrs. Yeats was out there, too, I knew. With a scholarship that could still be mine, a future at Benedict's, and—I thought with a pang—the only guy who'd ever made me sizzle. I'd only known Devon a few weeks, but my heart didn't seem to care. It just . . . ached. I'd done my best not to think about any of it over the past few days, but it all flooded through me now—everything I stood to lose.

My legs felt heavy climbing the steps. One. Two. Three. I still couldn't catch my breath—not surprising since my heart was racing out of control. I stood in the heat of the spotlights and shivered. I propped my bag behind the podium and gathered another breath.

The rows of people had turned into a shadow of black. In the sixth row, I knew, Mrs. Lee sat with the other judges. She'd been amazing. I'd called to tell her about Zeydeh, and I ended up telling her everything. *Everything.* She excused me from camp, offered to help if she could, and promised me a spot for the tourney. "Do this for yourself," she'd told me.

But I wasn't thinking of me. I was thinking of Mrs. Yeats. One of the things a good orator always considers is her audience. If you could target your speech to your audience, you'd have more success. And I had targeted my speech. But my audience of one wasn't going to love it. She was going to hate it.

She was going to hate me.

Or was she?

The tongue is the pen of the heart. It was another one of Zeydeh's favorite sayings and it flitted through my mind. If I spoke from the heart, I could do it. I could get through to her. And maybe, I could still have the dream. With that thought flowing through me like adrenaline, I took a breath and began:

"I haven't even said a word yet, and most of you have already judged me." I looked around the auditorium. "Maybe you had me figured out by the time I climbed these stairs. I'm a girl, after all. My speech is bound to be more emotional, right?"

I held out my arms and did a slow turn. "And look at the way I'm dressed." My skirt reached just above my knees, and the black lace camisole I'd borrowed from Megan hugged tight to my stomach and barely stretched across the padded bra I'd worn. "If you're showing cleavage, you can't be too smart, right? Though," I added, "I've got brown hair—which means I can't be a dumb blonde."

I smiled like we were all in on the same joke. "Come on, admit it. We all judge each other on appearances and it's harmless, right?"

I reached into my bag and pulled out a white shawl with

a beautiful pattern embroidered along the edges. I held it up. "But what if I had walked on stage wearing this shawl? You might have a completely different image of who I am." I wrapped the wide shawl over my shoulders, covering myself completely.

"What if I tell you this isn't any ordinary shawl? It belongs to my grandfather, Samuel Morris Levine. It's his tallis—his Jewish prayer shawl." I paused again. You could hear a fly flap its wings, it had gotten so quiet. "Does this change anything? Does this change everything?

"It shouldn't," I said matter-of-factly. "We all know stereotypes are wrong. Racism, bigotry, discrimination are old news. This is the twenty-first century, right? Heck, we've even elected an African American president." I paused. "The fact is, stereotypes of all kinds are still alive and well. Asians are good musicians. African Americans are good athletes. Beautiful people are shallow. Fat people are lazy. Guys who don't play sports are gay. Goths are druggies. We tell dumb-blonde jokes and Polish jokes and Jewish jokes and Irish jokes. And we tell ourselves they're harmless.

"I mean, why get all bent out of shape over a joke? Quit being so sensitive. What's the big deal?" I shrugged, then continued more softly. "So we keep quiet. We conform. We hide our true selves. And our true voices. We convince ourselves it doesn't matter. And this, I intend to argue, is the greatest problem we face. Not the prejudice itself, but the way we accept it, live with it, and enable it to continue. It does matter," I said. I stabbed the podium with a finger as I emphasized each word.

"It. Does. Matter. If we are truly to become the greatest generation ever, then the smallest injustice is big enough to stand against."

I moved across the stage then, moving into the main body of my oratory. I quoted statistics showing that hate groups were on the rise in America. I spoke about peer pressure and issues of self-esteem and the way society expects us to conform. If my voice shook when I spoke about acceptance and rejection, it was because I was close to tears and I couldn't help it. And I didn't really care. I didn't want to silence even that part of me. I spoke from the heart until finally, I found the center of the spotlight for one last thought.

My heart thudded. My muscles tensed and my insides contracted as if I were drawing myself in, giving it everything I had. "So today," I said, in a voice strong and sure, "when you judge me, judge me as a person. Judge me not on our differences but on our similarities. And I will pledge to do the same, knowing the most difficult thing in the world is for us to be ourselves—but that is exactly who we must be."

I finished with a sigh, and a wave of relief that made my legs feel weak. Applause reached me, a swell of sound that pulsed through me like a heartbeat. I'd done it! I'd done what I set out to do. I let the sound wash over me. It felt like more than appreciation tonight. It felt like support. For my message. For me.

I wondered . . . I couldn't help hoping . . . was Mrs. Yeats applauding, too?

◇

The judges took forty minutes to come to a decision.

Megan saw them come in and grabbed my wrist. "They're back," she whispered.

We'd gathered in the front corner, my family and the Swans. Other kids had done the same—found a corner or a row to hang out and wait. I think we were all too nervous to talk with each other until we knew.

And now we would.

I started back to my seat, only half feeling all the hands patting my back. Of course my family thought I'd won it all. Zeydeh had practically danced himself into another faint. I laughed with everyone else, not caring that he looked like Tevye from *Fiddler on the Roof.* I'd already outed him myself. And he loved it.

I kept my back toward the far corner where Devon and his family stood. But I couldn't stop thinking about Dynamite Doris. I guess I'd know soon enough.

Mrs. Lee led the judges back in. I was careful not to look at their faces, careful to keep my fingers crossed tightly. If I had won, I'd take my trophy and I'd find Doris Yeats and I'd make everything all right.

Okay, God? Deal?

Mrs. Lee took the stage and stood behind the podium. She smiled widely. "I want to thank everyone for being here tonight. We've witnessed some amazing performances. It's been a pleasure to work with your children during the past month."

The audience applauded loudly, then Mrs. Lee went on.

"Without any further ado, it's my pleasure to announce our top three winners. In third place, Andrew Sawyer."

Andrew stood up, beaming, and looking dazed for the first time ever. He jogged up the stairs to loud applause. Mrs. Lee shook his hand and presented him with a silver medal on a red ribbon.

"In second place," she continued, "Devon Yeats."

Again, thunderous applause. I clapped until my palms stung, but inside me, it felt like a blender whirled through my stomach. Had I won it all—or not even placed?

"And tonight's winner of the CSSPA Best in Original Oratory: Miss Eleanor Taylor."

It took my brain a second to believe my ears. It was Zeydeh's huge shout from behind that started my heart beating again. I felt hands on my back, pushing me up, and then I was standing, my knees barely holding steady. I walked to the stage, but it all felt unreal and dizzy. I never even felt the stairs under my feet, as if I were riding an escalator of clouds.

Mrs. Lee beamed as she handed me the trophy. "Congrats, Ellie!" She pulled me into a hug. "We'll talk later," she whispered.

I nodded, still dazed, pretty sure this would all sink in by next year sometime. I took a quick bow, then walked back down.

I got mobbed at the stairs. Everyone had stood, and Tammy, Sarah, and Nancy surrounded me with more hugs. From there, I got pulled into hugs with my family—a shoulder pat from Benny—and a huge squeeze from Megan. It felt like everyone was there.

But deep down, a part of me was keeping track. A part of me knew not *everyone* was there. Even surrounded as I was, I still felt a gap, a hole, from the one person who didn't come to congratulate me. Devon. Not that I was surprised. He had to stand with his family now. I'd just spoken out against his grandmother's beliefs, even if the rest of the audience didn't know it. Maybe Devon could never forgive me. Or accept me. The thought hurt.

So much for my speech about the importance of accepting ourselves.

By the time I'd finished showing off my trophy, the auditorium was nearly empty. The lobby had been set up with a dessert reception, and everyone would be stuffing their faces with cream puffs and brownies by now. Benny had dragged Dad and Zeydeh with him a few minutes ago. Mom had stayed to help fold up the tallis and pack up the rest of my things.

"You ready?" Mom asked.

I nodded. I was ready, but there was still one thing I had to do. I looked again at the trophy in my hands. It was shaped like a podium and it weighed enough to be made of solid gold. Next week, they'd engrave my name on the base. My name, like Zeydeh's, etched into history. But even without the engraving, it was official. I'd done it. I'd proven myself best of the best.

And maybe I'd proven something else. It was time to find out. I straightened up and lifted my shoulders. Toward the back, the judges were still hanging out with Mrs. Doris Yeats. "There's something I have to do, Mom," I said. "I'll see you in the lobby, okay?"

Before I could talk myself out of it, I started walking. Mrs. Yeats said I reminded her of herself—so she'd have to see the strength and courage it took tonight and respect me for it. I turned up the main aisle and hefted the trophy in my hand, feeling the solid weight. Everything else tonight had gone right. This would, too.

She stood a few rows up, talking with one of the other judges—an older man with a round, smiling face and a huge gap between his two front teeth. I couldn't hear the conversation, but I relaxed when I heard her laugh. She didn't sound mad. A second later, the man kissed her on the cheek, then headed out. And Doris Yeats turned to me.

In the split second it took for her to recognize my face, I knew.

CHAPTER 33

I'd always thought of hate as a feeling. Now, I realized it was also an expression. Her features turned rigid, like wet concrete hardening into stone. Only her eyes were alive, and those were an icy blue, so cold they burned.

I stumbled back a step, the warm triumph of the night burning into a layer of sweat on my skin. "I . . . I just wanted to explain."

Her eyes narrowed. "I think you've said enough."

"But I want you to understand."

Her gaze swept over me like I was some kind of nasty bug. "Oh, I do. You're not who I hoped you were."

I've only been slapped once in my life. I was five and Benny was three. We fought the way only brothers and sisters can. We pinched and poked and grabbed and yanked. I was older and bigger and I liked to win even back then. The fights always ended with me victorious and Benny in tears.

Until one day, I reached for a chunk of his hair, and he slapped me. Hard.

It was a lucky hit. His flailing hand accidentally slid past my arm and landed smack on my cheekbone. I fell back, almost stunned with the pain. But worse than the sting and burn was the shock. I hadn't seen it coming.

That's exactly how I felt now. Doris's hands were still by her sides, but it felt like she'd slapped me. I wanted to fall back. I wanted to cry. Mostly, I didn't want it to hurt so much.

"I'm sorry," I managed. I stepped back, needing to escape—and felt two arms reach out to steady me.

I felt the heat of his touch and nearly let out a cry. *Devon!*

I turned and his eyes, those same eyes as his grand-mother's, were guarded but warm. I swallowed, too full of tears to say anything.

"You okay?" he asked.

I nodded.

"Good-bye, Miss Taylor," Mrs. Yeats said in a low voice. "And know that you go with nothing. Not my respect, and certainly not my money. Who do you think you are to lec-ture me?"

"Grandmother," Devon said, a pleading note in his voice.

I blinked back tears and faced her. "I don't want your money." An edge of the trophy dug into my palm, reminding me that what I'd won was more important than what I'd lost. I lifted the trophy to my heart and held it there. "That's what I came to tell you. I just wanted to change your mind—even a little."

"Oh, you did," she said. "I know now you're nothing like me. Obviously, it was all a lie for the scholarship. A Jew through and through," she mocked.

"Grandmother, stop!" Devon stepped in front of me. "It's not right to say that. And Ellie didn't lie. She told me the truth from the beginning. I was the one who said religion shouldn't matter."

"You've been fooled, Devon." Doris's cheeks flushed red, but her eyes were still cold. "And make no mistake: whatever your friendship was, it's over." She leaned past Devon to meet my eyes, her chest rising with her words. "Your connection with this family—all members of it—is over."

Before I could say anything, Devon shook his head. His chin stuck out in a way I'd never seen before. "That's not up to you."

Doris Yeats drew herself up. "You and I will speak about this later," she said sharply. Then she turned her death stare on me. "Let me save you a trip back tomorrow for the awarding of the scholarship. You are the last student I would ever select."

She started to push her way past, expecting us to move. But I wasn't going anywhere. I was done hiding. I shifted to block the aisle.

Her eyes flashed fire. "Get out of my way."

"I've listened to you," I said. "Now you can listen to me."

"Do you see the arrogance?" she said to Devon.

I sucked in a breath—the air felt poisoned with her words. But I forced myself to go on, too angry to be afraid. "I was wrong not to tell the whole truth. And for that, I am really sorry."

"I don't care."

"I don't care if you care," I retorted. "But in my religion, we're taught to admit our mistakes and to apologize for them." I started to turn away, and then stopped. "Oh, and there's one other thing I'm sorry about," I added. "I should've spit in your eye and called you a *szhlob* weeks ago."

Then I stepped out of her way. When the door slammed shut behind her, it was just Devon and me.

Except . . . there was no more Devon and me.

CHAPTER 34

The hall was dark except for strips of emergency lights spaced along the ceiling. Devon raised the blinds around the window nook, and a nearly full moon gave the semicircle a pale yellow glow.

We sat across from each other like we had that first day. Like strangers. In the dark, I could barely see his eyes. Good. I didn't want to lose myself in a pair of baby blues ever again.

I didn't want to lose myself, period.

People were still sipping coffee and eating cream puffs in the lobby, but the noise didn't reach this far. It felt like we were the only two people left in the building. I'd found Mom to tell her where I was going. She stood with Jennifer Yeats, who grasped my hand and squeezed tightly when I walked up.

"Your speech was amazing, Ellie."

"Thank you," I said, sounding as stiff and wary as I felt.

Maybe she was like Doris. Maybe I was Public Enemy #1. But if I was, what was she doing squeezing my hand?

"I was saying to your mother it's a little startling to hear your children speak, and realize it's not your words they're repeating anymore." She sighed. "But I'll let Devon explain that."

Something else for us to talk about, I guess. And it had been his idea for us to talk. But neither of us seemed to know where to start. The silence felt thick around me. I'd put my jacket back on, and now I wrapped it around me, stretching the material like a blanket.

Devon had come to my defense, and even though that meant the world to me, I didn't know what it meant to him. All the ugly things I'd said to him at the hospital floated in front of me like dust in the air. I swallowed, gathering my courage. "I guess it's my night to apologize."

"No," he said. "I'm the one who's sorry."

His words made it easier for me to breathe. "I never meant it to turn out like this," I said, looking out the window at a clump of bushes, gray green in the moonlight. "I kept rationalizing why it was okay to hide my religion."

"I'm the one who told you to."

"But I did it." I traced a finger over the glass. "I shouldn't have blamed you." I finally met his eyes. "At the hospital."

"You were worried about your grandpa."

"I still shouldn't have done it."

"It's okay."

"It isn't."

His lips suddenly twitched into a smile.

"What?"

"You," he said. "You're arguing again."

I had to smile a little at that. "Thank you for tonight, Devon. For standing up for me."

"I should have done it sooner." He leaned forward, resting his elbows on his knees. "You were right, all the things you said at the hospital. And during your oratory. It felt like you were talking to me."

"I thought I could get through to your grandmother."

"I should have helped."

"No." I shook my head. "It was my fight."

"Maybe it should be all of our fights."

I picked at a thread on my jacket. "That's a really cool thing to say. But I'm guessing it's not so easy when it's your grandmother."

"I told myself it was just a business thing, you know? Not a racist thing." He shrugged. "Then you basically called me a wimp at the hospital." He glanced up at me. "Totally pissed me off, by the way."

He sat back, stretching out his legs. "When I got home, my mom had made meat loaf for dinner. She'd put a plate in the fridge for me, and she wanted to warm it up. I started yelling at her about meat loaf, how I hate meat loaf. She makes meat loaf all the time, and I always eat it, but suddenly I'm shouting that it looks like a slice of dog poop and doesn't taste much better."

I made a face. "Bet that went over well."

"I didn't care about the stupid meat loaf," he said. "I was mad because of you. Because you were right. I don't speak up for myself and I'd been eating meat loaf forever because it was my dad's favorite, and I'd let my mom think it was my favorite, too."

"So what did your mom say?"

"She stared for a really long time at the plate of meat loaf and then she asked, 'You don't like Caesar salad either, do you?'"

I smiled at the dryness in his voice. "Another one of your dad's favorites?"

He met my eyes, smiling with me. "It got easier after that. We worked our way from desserts to dad's favorite kind of socks, and finally to oratory."

I raised my eyebrows. "And?"

"She cried."

"Oh, Devon—"

"No," he said, interrupting me, "it was actually okay. In a weird way, it was good it happened. She still wishes I'd follow in my dad's footsteps, but she's cool with some detours." He grinned. "I've already talked to Mrs. Lee about doing radio broadcast at Benedict's."

"Really?"

He nodded. "I owe you for that."

"I figured you must hate me."

"No."

He said it so fast, my heart thumped quicker. "You never called," I said.

"I didn't know you wanted me to." He sighed. "Besides, what could I say? That you were right and I wasn't?" He ran a hand through his hair. "Who wants to say that?"

I smiled.

"Camp didn't feel right without you. Nothing did."

I blushed so hard, I could feel my ears tingle. "What about your grandmother?"

"She's still my grandmother. But she's not telling me who I can be with."

I looked back out at the night. "You won't see me once school starts, anyway."

He leaned closer. "You deserve the scholarship, Ellie. You were awesome tonight."

"Well." I smiled, a teasing note in my voice. "At least I finally did it."

"What?"

"Kicked your butt."

"Don't get used to it." He grinned back. He shifted around the nook until he sat next to me. "I've always wanted a long-distance girlfriend."

"Is Canyon View long distance enough?"

He reached for my hand. I let him slip his palm in mine, loving the tiny sizzle that lifted the hairs along my neck. Then he kissed me. I lifted my arms around his neck and I kissed him back, and I knew maybe not everything was right in the world. But it felt pretty dang close.

◇◇◇◇◇

CHAPTER 35

The last day of camp was ending the way the first day had started: with a general assembly. Mrs. Clancy stood onstage, lips still pursed, face frozen into a look of disapproval as we slid into the rows.

I followed Megan just like on the first day—only now, Anna Hernandez was leading the way and Devon was following me, holding my hand. That first day, I'd dreamed of winning the oratory event. But I'd never dreamed of everything else that had happened.

Last night, and Devon.

This morning, and Mrs. Lee.

She'd asked me to meet with her a few minutes before class started. We'd settled into two chairs in the back of the computer lab. "I have something for you," she said. She slid a yellow manila envelope in front of me.

"What is it?" I asked. "A certificate?" But it felt too thick and heavy for that. I turned the envelope over in my hands, but there was no writing on it.

"Go ahead," she urged. "Open it."

I slid my finger under the flap and ripped it open. I pulled out some papers and recognized my handwriting. They were the admission forms I turned in when I applied for the Benedict's Scholarship. "Oh. I guess they don't need these anymore." I flashed her a smile and slid the papers back in. "Thanks." She probably didn't want to risk passing these back in class and watching me burst into tears.

"You will need those," she said softly, "along with the tuition-waiver forms."

I frowned, sure I'd heard her wrong. "What do you mean? What tuition waiver?"

"It's not a full scholarship," she said. "You'll need to cover books and other fees."

I shook my head, still not believing what she seemed to be saying. "I researched it, though. There are no tuition waivers."

"Not for incoming freshmen," she agreed. "But there are opportunities for exceptional transfer students."

A tremor raced through me. "Transfer students?"

"You would start high school at Canyon View, and then apply for a transfer. Tuition waivers are awarded at the discretion of the board," Mrs. Lee added, "which is why I spoke to a few members last week. I explained your situation and invited them to attend our final tournament."

I stared at the envelope that held my future. "You did this?"

"No, Ellie," she said seriously. "You did this. You're the one who took the stage last night. You won the tournament, and you won a great deal of respect. That's why I'll be recommending you for this waiver, and why the board will agree."

"I don't believe it," I whispered.

Her eyes met mine. "When you speak up, you never know who might be listening."

I pulled the envelope closer, curling my fingers around the edge. "What about Mrs. Yeats? Isn't she a member of the board?"

Mrs. Lee waved a hand in the air. "Mrs. Yeats's involvement and influence only extend so far. Especially when her actions fail to reflect the mission of the school. I can promise you, Ellie, that Jewish people feel very welcome at Benedict's." She smiled. "At least, I do."

I gasped. "You're Jewish?"

"I sure am." She patted the envelope. "So go through the packet with your parents. If you work hard and maintain at least a B-plus average, you can start Benedict's after Christmas break."

"You mean Hanukkah break," I corrected.

We both laughed.

"Thank you," I finally said, my throat tightening up. I opened my mouth, then closed it, then opened it again. "I don't know what else to say."

"I'm sure that won't last for long." She grinned.

I still could hardly believe it. I'd told Megan, Anna, and Devon. I couldn't wait to get home to tell Mom, Dad, and especially Zeydeh. There'd be a short delay, but I was going to

◇◇◇◇◇

Benedict's—me, Eleanor Jane Taylor. And I was going to make that name mean something.

Mrs. Clancy quieted everyone, and began with a round of thanks to all the team leaders and administrators. "And now, I'd like you to give your attention to Mrs. Doris Yeats, who will announce the winner of the Benedict's Scholarship."

She strode to the podium, wearing a gray suit with a red blouse. I could hardly look at her, so I didn't. I looked at my lap, where my hand was circled in Devon's. I couldn't block out her voice, but that was okay, because after a lot of garbage about the talented crop of students, she said, "I am proud to award one scholarship this year to a most deserving student: Miss Anna Hernandez."

Anna jumped up, her hands clapped over her mouth. Megan and I glanced at each other, then burst into loud applause as Anna ran to the stage and accepted the certificate with a bow. Then she pretended to faint. I laughed. Megan was going to have some competition for the title of Drama Queen.

"And now," Mrs. Clancy said, "let us bow our heads."

I watched everyone bow their heads, and then I tilted up my face. Somewhere up there, God was looking out for me. So was Bubbe, and Great-Grandma Eleanor, and everyone else. Which was good, because I was going to need some help. I'd have a lot of butts to kick as a member of the Benedict's speech team.

I grinned, closed my eyes, and sent up my own prayer. *What a day, huh, God? I still can't believe it all. But I know I couldn't have done it alone. So thanks for being you. And thanks for making me . . . be me.*

◇◇◇◇◇

ACKNOWLEDGMENTS

◇◇◇◇◇

A special thanks to:

Erik Dominguez, coach of Desert Vista High School's Thunder Speech, Theater and Debate Company. I was fortunate to learn from and observe the best. (As of this writing in 2010, DV has won seven consecutive state championships!)

Bill Andrew, cofounder of the Summit School of Ahwatukee, who agreed to answer a few questions and ended up answering a few hundred.

My family and friends, including Sue, my sounding board; Daphne, who read two years of rough drafts; Dorothy, who had answers for all my odd questions; and Kyle, for reading each chapter as I wrote it and asking for more.

A heartfelt thanks to my agent, Caryn Wiseman, for seeing the potential in a first page. And to my editor, Stacy Cantor Abrams, for her insight and care in bringing this book to life.

Finally, and most especially, to Jake. For always believing.